Spice for my Santa

LYNN JOSEPH

BLACK MERMAID PRESS
BOOKS THAT CHALLENGE THE STATUS QUO

For all my Caribbean Christmas lovers!

St. Nicholas Island

In the entryway of my mother's house in upstate New York, there is a portrait of me and my mother.

We're at a park. I'm swinging high into the sky on a wooden swing. My mom is standing in the background. Her face is a mixture of joy and worry.

The artist said it was the perfect portrayal of motherhood. He won a few prizes for that drawing.

Now, on this Thanksgiving Day, I am standing in the hallway staring at that portrait he gifted to Mom.

It tells me nothing of how I should feel as I wait for the child I gave birth to nineteen years ago to knock on the door and introduce herself to me and her grandmother.

Nineteen years is a long time. A lot has happened and changed during that time.

I'm far from being that college student at Howard University hiding a secret pregnancy from her family and friends.

A family in Virginia adopted my beautiful daughter. I have no right to call her my "daughter," and in my head, I refer to her as "the child I gave birth to," so I don't allow myself any leeway in thinking I have any right to claim her as my own.

I do not.

Years of revisiting that painful and lonely time in my head have not lessened the blame I felt and still feel. I am undeserving of her company, her attention, and most definitely, her love.

My heart squeezes at the memory. And until recently, I didn't believe I deserved anyone's love at all after giving up my child to strangers.

Yes, they'd love and care for her as their child. But I always wondered if she believed her birth mother didn't love her.

I am waiting now for that doorbell to ring. I've prepared myself internally and externally for whatever comes my way.

But still...my heart hammers with nerves. I clutch my hands tightly. Excitement and fear ripple through every bit of my body.

I glance in the hallway mirror for the hundredth time. My eyes are huge in my face. My brown skin looks grey with worry.

My bottom lip is bruised from me biting it.

My phone beeps. I grab it, thinking it might be her.

It isn't. It's my love, Keston Kips. The man who helped me believe in miracles. Like the one that is happening to me right now.

"Baby, I'm thinking of you. I took off work to wait by my phone. Call me for any reason. I wish I could be there holding your hand. You deserve all the love in the world. Remember that."

A tiny sob catches in my throat.

He'd have been here at my side if the U.S. visa had come through in time.

But he's in my heart and spirit. Always.

"Thank you," I type back.

I square my shoulders.

"Are you crying, Carmela Jones?" My mother walks over with a look that is neither joy nor worry.

I can't detect what she's feeling. My mother is an enigma. She's a demanding professor of English literature at LaSalle University in our town. I used to fear her.

I still do, even though I'm a forty-year-old woman.

I wonder if I'll ever stop being afraid of my mother—her opinions, judgment, and expectations. She expected me to be an upstanding citizen and a person dedicated to justice, which is why I became a lawyer—to make her happy.

A career I followed for almost twenty years.

Now, along with meeting my daughter, whom my mother was appalled to discover I had kept hidden for twenty years, she's dealing with the fact that I have resigned from my job.

Yes, I finally did it. It's official. I am unemployed.

When I fell in love with Keston Kips and went back to St. Nicholas Island in the Caribbean to see if I could live there, no one, especially my mother, thought I'd actually decide to relocate there.

My friends know how whiny I can be and how much I enjoy my comfortable life in New York, with all the perks and glamour of being a new partner in a top law firm.

However, I felt less and less happy that I was working so much and not starting a family.

Which is where Keston Kips comes in.

As I recently discovered, everyone deserves a life they never dreamed possible. True love can do more than throw you off course. It can revitalize you and propel you into a second chapter.

Which is what I am calling this new path. My second chapter.

So, here I am, ready for Chapter 2 to begin.

Before I can settle fully into my new home on St. Nicholas Island, I am here in New York to meet this amazing daughter—the girl/woman who found me.

And to be in her life in whatever capacity she chooses.

"Bzzzzzzz."

The doorbell chimes. My heart flies to my throat. My stomach clenches. My hand reaching for the doorknob is shaking so badly I have to hold the knob with two hands.

This is harder than surviving a hurricane. Or slaying a sea beast.

But it's also as momentous as meeting your true love on a hillside overlooking the sea when the sky is full of stars, and you have nothing to lose.

Because I am meeting my Lucy.

Two weeks ago, I was in a hammock on the front porch of what Keston now calls "our home" on the beach. I was lost in thought, imagining how this very moment would unfold.

Me and Lucy. Face to face.

Would we hug warmly?

Kiss each other's cheeks politely?

Or run into each other's arms like long-lost family?

I would have wanted that last one, but it was highly unlikely.

"What do you think, Kes? You think she'll like me?"

Keston was busy cutting bamboo strips for the giant kite he was making. He'd stop and push my hammock every few minutes to keep my momentum going.

"Um, sweetie," I murmured as my hammock slowed down.

He shoved the hammock with one hand while bending the bamboo with his other.

"I think she'll find you fascinating."

I frowned.

"She's not you."

"Nobody's me," he said matter-of-factly. And he was right.

"I mean, she's not in love with me."

"Not yet," he said, also matter-of-factly.

I bit my bottom lip. "What if she asks me hard questions I can't answer?"

He bit a bamboo strip and yanked it through his teeth, splitting it into the thinnest shreds.

"Ha! That'll be the day you don't have an answer for something."

I sucked my teeth the rude way the islanders do.

"Finally," he muttered, flipping the delicate kite frame around. "This one will be so light, it'll float like a butterfly."

I watched in utter fascination as he took scraps of nothing and molded them into a beautiful piece of art.

He was making what had to be his tenth kite of the day when I sat up.

All around the porch was a line of beautiful kites in different sizes, colors, and designs.

Some were shaped like diamonds, and some had shiny decorations that I later learned were pieces of chewing gum silver wrappers.

"You can't fly that kite, babe," I said, pointing to the one in his hand. "It's too beautiful."

He snorted. "That's the point. It has to be attractive and aerodynamic. Kind of like you."

He had the nerve to wink.

A loud groan escaped me. "I swear you must be the corniest cool guy I've ever met."

To prove my point, he kissed my forehead as he stood up to place his latest creation next to the others.

"I'll fly this one in the competition," he said. "Since it's your favorite."

"I want to use it for a wall decoration. We can use them all. Your house needs art on the walls. These are perfect."

"It's *our* house, missy. But what will I fly?"

I shrugged. "I don't know. Make an ugly one."

He tapped my leg with a bamboo stick. "I want to win."

"It's just a kite contest." I rolled my eyes. "How serious is it?"

"Are you kidding me? This is our national celebration."

"Right. St. Nicholas Day. When is it again? Christmas day?"

"You're one of us now. You should know when we celebrate our island's special day."

I racked my brain to see if I could recall St. Nicholas Day being a particular day.

He shoved my hammock extra hard. "Maybe that will jostle some of your brain cells."

"Meanie."

I swatted his arm or tried to when my hammock swung toward him.

He grinned. "We can practice."

"Practice what?"

"Me asking you hard questions you can't answer."

My body slumped into the soft hemp of the hammock that Keston's brother Kelley made as a gift for me. To thank me for saving his life.

Keston's tone softened. "St. Nicholas's Day is December 6th. We celebrate all over the island. Will you be back for it?"

"I'm going for Thanksgiving and coming right back. So yes. Do you also celebrate Christmas Day?"

"We do. On December 25th." He eyed me suspiciously. "But when is St. Nicholas Day again?"

I roll my eyes. "If you aren't nicer to me, I won't give you any of that sweet thing you love before I leave."

This time, it was he who snorted. "You mean I won't have to fight you off my body?"

My fingers snapped in his face as my hammock rolled toward him. "You can beg, and I still won't do it."

"Ha! We'll see about that." As my hammock swung toward him again, he tipped it high up, and I tumbled into his waiting arms.

He kissed my shoulders and ripped down my top with his bamboo-stripping teeth.

"What are you doing?" I squealed.

"You're being a naughty girl again, CJ. Time for your punishment."

"You punished me this morning already."

A gleam of mischief filled his dark brown eyes. "That was four hours ago."

I pushed him away. "You have kites to make. And I have to figure out what I will say to my daughter when I meet her. This is nerve-wracking."

"You're worrying too much. But if I were you, I'd get her a present. Something small and sweet."

I leaped up. "You're right. Something beautiful but made with love."

He nodded. "Exactly."

I grabbed his hands. "You're a genius, Kes. I love you so much."

The smile on his face lifted my heart.

I gently picked up the last perfect kite he made. "This will be just the gift for her."

He smacked his forehead. "Me and my dumb ideas."

I laughed merrily. "Maybe she and I can fly it together."

The scowl on Keston's face was quickly replaced with a big smile of love. "Anything for you, baby."

I felt a sense of peace and gratitude. I was one lucky woman to have a man like Keston Kips looking out for me.

I only hoped I would remember this feeling when the time came to meet the young woman of my dreams.

The baby girl I never forgot — not one single day of my life.

Chapter Three

That feeling of peace is like a snowflake hitting a radiator.

Or a kite being swept away by the north wind.

Poof! It's gone the minute I woke up this morning and

dressed in what I hoped were age-appropriate mother-type clothes.

"What the hell are you wearing?" my mother snapped.

I spun around in the hallway mirror.

"You look like you're appearing before the Senate for your nomination to the Supreme Court bench. Not that that could happen anymore," she ended sadly.

"I want to look . . ."

"Responsible? That ship sailed a long time ago."

"Mom, I'm nervous."

She sipped her tea and fiddled with her earrings.

Maybe I wasn't the only one who was nervous.

We spent the morning setting the table, checking on the turkey, and baking pies.

Now, at the sound of the buzzer, Mom appears at my elbow. "Open it already before she leaves."

I yank open the door and gasp.

My gorgeous daughter is covered in light, silvery snowflakes. They dot her eyelashes and light up her dark brown curly hair that resembles mine.

Tears spring to my eyes. It's like looking in a mirror.

I hear a loud intake of breath from behind my shoulder. Mom must also recognize the resemblance.

"It's snowing," says the angel in front of me. Her brown eyes dart from me to my mother.

"Hi, I'm Lucy."

The snow blows sideways into my eyes. I feel the world tilting upside down. To my great embarrassment, my knees give way.

I have fought for my life through a dangerous hurricane

and faced off with a giant green eel the size of the Loch Ness monster, yet I collapse like a bag of potatoes.

"Mom?"

"Carmela?"

"Get her inside, quick," says my mother.

Two strong arms reach for me.

It's the hug I longed for. Except not under these circumstances.

The strong young woman half carries me inside the house and settles me into one end of our velvet sofa.

"I'm so sorry," she says, picking up one of my hands and checking for my pulse.

I hear her sweet voice say, "I'm studying pre-med."

"Of course you are, you beautiful child," my mother says, sweeping her up in a giant hug. They forget all about me.

I watch them as if I'm on the ceiling, looking down at the scene.

Mom hugs and kisses her in a way she never did with me.

Lucy laughs in her embrace.

It feels right. Seeing them together like this.

My mom is a real mother. She knows all the right things to say and do.

While I, on the other hand, am nothing but an imposter.

Chapter Four

I'm a firm believer in being prepared. A necessity when practicing before some of the crankiest judges in the New York legal system.

But nothing could have equipped me for this meeting.

Some moments in your life will take your breath away

and turn your world upside down in ways you can never anticipate.

Moments like falling in love.

Or meeting your child for the first time.

The only thing you can do is try your damnest to stay grounded, focused, and ... in my case ... at least *conscious*!

"I'm sorry," I say as I swing my legs to the floor and stand up shakily.

I make my way into the kitchen to find my Mom and Lucy chatting about Lucy's interest in pre-med as they press fork tines along the edges of the pie crusts.

Lucy may resemble me in her features, but she is uniquely herself in every other way. For one thing, she is poised. No fainting for her.

She exudes confidence and knowledge. Like she can do anything. Bake a pie or fly a plane in an emergency.

Or catch her fainting birth mother before she hits the cold, snowy cement.

Now, she carefully puts her fork on the counter and looks at me.

That's when I notice the flicker of nervousness. Her brown eyes look into mine, then dart away.

I swallow hard.

"Speak, you fool!" I shout at myself in my head. "Don't let her think she came all this way for nothing."

If there's anything I have learned from Keston Kips, it's to say what you feel. Don't hesitate, even if it sounds dumb in your head. Speak your heart—like he does.

"Hello, Lucy," my voice cracks. I clear my throat.

"Hi," she says softly.

"Can I. . . . um . . . give you a hug?"

In truth, I want to snatch her up in my arms and never let her go, but this is not the time to act impulsively.

Mom mumbles something about checking the dining room table and exits the kitchen.

Lucy steps toward me and opens her arms. I wrap my arms around her, feel the warmth of her body, and inhale the sweet, flowery scent of her shampoo.

OMG, I'm hugging my daughter. All that fancy talk about not calling her *my* daughter flies out the window.

She's taller than me, but she drops her head onto my shoulder at the exact time I say, "You feel the same. I hugged you a lot the day you were born."

A sob giggle escapes my throat. "I'm sorry. I'm not trying to be overly sentimental about this. I'm thrilled that you came to meet us."

When we step away from each other's embrace, I tell her honestly, "I have thought about you every day of your life. And I . . . I am so sorry . . . ."

Her dark curls shake side to side, illuminating a lavender spiral of hair. I want to reach out and touch it.

"You're so beautiful," I whisper instead.

"My parents told me all the time I was their greatest gift. Thanks to you."

I smile shakily.

"It's a lot of pressure being someone's greatest gift, let me tell you." She laughs, and I see straight teeth from years of orthodontics and hear glee mixed with teenage aggravation.

"There's a star in the galaxy made out of real diamonds called Lucy," I tell her. "Do you know it?"

She shakes her curls. Some more of her lavender curls light up like a unicorn's mane.

"I love looking at the stars, though," she says quickly. "Is that something you like to do?"

I nod. "My boyfriend Keston Kip's favorite hobby. He makes me look at them with this ancient telescope. I keep offering to buy him a new one, but he says we shouldn't replace things that are working perfectly fine to have a newer model."

Am I rambling? Do I sound as if I'm bragging about my great boyfriend? Oh God. Suppose she thinks I'm this boy-crazy woman. As ditzy as when I was twenty-one.

"Is that the guy whose life you saved?" Lucy slides onto a stool.

"Twice," I say, holding up two fingers. "I think I've earned his complete devotion."

"I couldn't believe the stories I read about you online. That was incredible. I had to meet you. Was it scary?"

I have a flashback of being stuck on No Man's Land and almost dying in the hurricane.

"It was. But totally worth it if it made you want to meet me."

Her pretty, unblemished skin puckers into a deep frown.

"I should have called you," she says. "Then you wouldn't have had to risk your life to get my attention."

I swat a hand in the air.

"Mom says I like to do things the hard way."

"Me too, actually," she smiles. "My mother calls me a drama queen."

An awkward silence follows.

I hurry over to the coffee machine. "Tell me the last time she told you that. What were you doing?"

I am busy with my hands trying to figure out Mom's complicated coffee machine.

She comes back in and shoos me away.

"Do you drink coffee?" Mom asks Lucy.

"I'm more of an espresso person."

My entire body tingles. "Me too!"

"So we're both drama queens who like espresso," Lucy chuckles.

My mother stares at me, then Lucy, and back again. A small smile curls her lips.

"I'll just be here drinking hot, boring coffee and finishing the turkey. You girls can go to the Starbucks and get espressos."

I blink. "Really? You wouldn't mind, Mom."

I turn to Lucy. "It's a ten-minute walk. We can bundle up and get there before they close early for the holiday."

"I'm down," she says. "Can we get anything for you . . . ." She looks at my Mom.

You can tell she's not sure what to call my mother, whose name is Annie. Maybe she was considering calling her 'grandma.'

Mom's entire face lights up. Even her eyes glow with a ridiculous sparkle.

She puts down the thermometer she was using to stab the turkey.

"You can call me Annie. Or anything you want."

Lucy nods. "Thanks . . . Annie."

Mom nods. "Perfect. Now, get going. Carmela, please put on your boots. It's slippery out there."

I roll my eyes. "Yes, Mom."

Lucy giggles. "I suppose we're always children to our parents." She stops dead in her tracks, and her face pales. "I didn't mean . . . ."

She looks so stricken that I feel sorry for her. "You didn't say anything wrong. Mom treats me like I'm twelve all the time."

Mom shakes her turkey baster at us. "That's because she acts twelve. Now go on."

Chapter Five

Mom's idea to walk outside in the snowy weather was genius. Under normal circumstances, I wouldn't be caught dead out here. I'd be inside next to the fireplace, reading a romance novel and complaining to Mom about the lack of rich, dark chocolate in her house.

But walking beside Lucy through the falling snowflakes, the world looks like Stars Hollow, and I feel very Gilmore Girls. Me and my daughter.

"Are you very close to your parents?" I venture.

I'm unsure what's safe territory for conversation, but I figure I'll be my authentic self and ask the questions I'm dying to know the answers to.

Lucy catches snowflakes on her mittens. I watch her watch them melt away, her eyes as bright as the snow.

A terrible ache hits my gut.

"I've missed all the magical moments in your life," I blurt without realizing.

Her hands tug her wool cap down on her curls. "I hope I have a lot more magical moments."

"Of course you will," I say quickly.

We reach Main Street.

As we turn the corner to head down the street I've known most of my life, someone hits the switch and holiday lights illuminate the entire area.

Trees twinkle above us, storefronts glow with festive wreaths and ribbons, and teddy bears with presents in their hands dance along the window sills.

"Oh wow!" we both exclaim.

Lucy and I look at each other and grin.

"See," she says. "Magic moments."

"Thank you for being here to share this with me."

She takes off her mittens as we enter the Starbucks and

line up to order. There's a surprisingly long line for Thanksgiving Day.

"We're not the only ones craving our "usual." I wave to some long time LaSalle residents.

Oh God. I hope no one asks me who Lucy is. I'm not prepared for the explanation.

She looks around with her bright robin eyes. "You're well-known huh?"

I shake my head. "No. They all know my mother. Annie is the star. Once I left for the big city, I became the dying star that doesn't give off light anymore."

"Like a white dwarf," says Lucy.

"Huh?"

She sighs. "I'm a nerd. A white dwarf is a dying star."

"Oh," I smile at my brilliant daughter. "I'll tell Keston. Hehehe."

A sweet giggle escapes her. "You're pretty funny."

"My boyfriend would beg to differ."

We reach the head of the line and give our orders.

I get a double espresso latte. Lucy orders a holiday drink with steamed oat milk, gingerbread, and other fancy ingredients.

"It's like a present in a cup," she whispers to me. "I get one when it's a special day.

I beam.

"Or when I'm really down."

I bite my lower lip, wondering which category her holiday drink falls into right now.

We're lucky to grab two tall stools together. For the next

five minutes, we sit and stare at the drifting snowflakes and sip our hot espresso drinks.

The silence is swallowed up by the Christmas carols playing over the speakers. For all intents and purposes, we're in a sweet Christmas Lifetime movie.

No drama. No tears. No accusations. It's almost too perfect.

After a while, I say, "My boyfriend taught me some great life lessons. One of them is not to look back with regret but to look forward and do better with the knowledge we have gained from mistakes."

Lucy stirs her incredibly aromatic drink. It smells like a cake.

I shake my head as if arguing with Keston Kips right here. "But I do have a regret. And I can't help but look back and think what I could have done differently."

I take a big sip of my drink to cover the tears threatening to leak from my eyes.

It's the damn *Silent Night* song blaring on the speakers. It's got me all up in my feelings.

"Well, why'd you do it? Why'd you put me up for adoption?"

My heart races. My foot taps a million miles an hour under the table. This is it. The beginning of the hard questions I feared.

I stare into my cup, wishing the mermaid logo would show itself in real life and help me out here.

Lucy's eyes are on me. She squares her shoulders as if bracing for the dumb answer I will give her.

I dig deep for the courage I need to face my daughter. My Lucy in the sky.

I inhale deeply. Press both hands hard on the tabletop. Don't you dare cry? I scold myself. This is not about you.

"I was . . . afraid."

I force myself to return in my mind to those months when I was twenty-one and pregnant and thinking I didn't have what it took to be anyone's mother.

"I was afraid I'd have to drop out of college. I was afraid my mother would be so angry she'd disown me. I was afraid I couldn't be a good mother to you. I was a big scaredy cat. And I am ashamed for the girl I was back then."

I release the breath I was holding.

Lucy stares out the plate glass window at the swirling snow.

"I was weak," I admit. "But I am not anymore," I say fiercely. "I'm here to be whatever you need me to be in your life. If you let me be in your life. I promise I will not let you down again."

As the song changes to *We Wish You a Merry Christmas*, Lucy turns large, dark eyes on me. I can't read what's in them.

Anger? Pity? Revulsion?

Her next words will be the most important of my life.

"I have amazing parents. If I were to get pregnant in college, they'd support me in every way."

My head dips low. "That's great, Lucy."

"You know what my adopted Mom said to me when I told her I was coming to meet you?"

I shake my head.

"She said no one can ever have too many people loving them. And if you wanted a chance to love me, I should give it to you."

My head shoots up. "What a wise person. And generous."

Lucy nods. "You picked a wonderful couple to raise me. Thank you. But I felt as if something was missing."

"Yes, me too. I always felt something was missing in my life from the day I gave you to them."

"How do you feel now?" Her voice is soft but strong. Like whatever I say, she can handle it.

I stand up and open my arms wide. "I feel as if I have arrived. Finally. In your life."

She pushes back her stool and enters my arms. We stand there wrapped up tightly, two curly-haired women reunited.

"You know what this means now, right?" Lucy says, leaning back and smiling at me.

Her entire face is awash in a glow of happiness. Mirroring mine, I am sure.

"What does it mean?"

"We've gotta find my birth dad."

I gulp. "About that . . . ."

Chapter Six

Getting back to St. Nicholas is easier said than done. First, I have to fly from New York to Miami.

Then wait for a few hours in the Miami airport. Then

catch my connecting flight to St. Nicholas, the beautiful Caribbean island where I met my true love.

I have plenty of time to think about how to help Lucy find her birth father.

It's a seemingly impossible task given that I was like the mother in *Mamma Mia*, who had slept with three different men and didn't know who the father was.

Except in my case, it could be more than three. Don't judge!

I'd rather think about our wonderful Thanksgiving dinner. After Lucy and I bonded over espressos, it was smooth sailing.

Mostly due to my Mom, who kept the conversation flowing with stories about me as a wannabe cheerleader who became the cheer manager instead.

"It wasn't my fault I couldn't do a split."

Mom rubbed my arm. "You were a great cheer manager."

Then, out of the blue, Lucy asked if I could compile a list of possibilities—men I had been with between October and December, approximately nine months before her August 2nd birthday.

Mom blanched.

I don't think we expected Lucy to be so blunt.

At the look on our faces, Lucy grinned. "That's Gen Z for you. Keeping it real. No time to waste. If it helps, in October 2005, *Twilight* was released. To give you a memory pocket," she said.

I perked up. "I loved *Twilight*."

"Obviously, you weren't reading much," my mom grumbled.

I slumped in my seat.

Lucy came to my defense. "I'm not trying to slut shame you."

At her use of the word "slut," my mom stood up, her face bright pink. "I'll go in the kitchen and get the desserts ready."

"I'm extremely embarrassed I can't tell you who your birth father is," I tell Lucy. "I wasn't discreet. I was all over the place. I was like a free bird in college. Maybe it was low self-esteem."

Lucy glanced up at me. "Do you know folks with ADHD have issues with promiscuous behaviors? It's one of the signs."

"Really? Maybe I have ADHD."

"It's hereditary. And I have it," Lucy says. "So it's a definite possibility."

I spin my dessert spoon on the table.

"Or I was just sexually overactive," I murmured. "I'm sorry I'm not very helpful."

Lucy takes out an iPad from her bag. "I've signed up for all the Ancestry sites. I bet I have a match one day. Everyone is doing it. A lot of adopted kids find their biological parents this way."

I was amazed at her resourcefulness. And determination.

This is why I scrolled through my old phone contacts while returning to St. Nicholas.

I had no clue who some of the names were.

Some names rang a bell, and memories of past dates popped into my head.

As much as I disliked this walk of shame down memory lane, I was determined to help my daughter.

One sexual memory at a time.

All I can say is that from now on, I will remember every sexual encounter I have—the who, what, when, where, how, and why.

And remember to take my birth control pills, too. Something I never forgot after that unexpected pregnancy.

Chapter Seven

When I land on St. Nicholas, Keston waits for me, holding a bouquet of wildflowers wrapped in a banana leaf and tied with a vine. The sunshine lights up every long eyelash on his gorgeous brown face. I bury my face in his chest and sigh as his arms wrap around me.

"It's okay, baby. I'm here."

I mumble incoherently.

"Did you say you're never leaving me again?" he laughs.

I roll my head side to side on his soft tee shirt. "Never."

"Good. From now on, invite everyone to come visit us."

I peep up from under my eyelashes. "I already did."

He hoots with laughter. "Perfect. When? Our wedding?"

I smack his arm and lean backward. "You have not proposed."

At his silence, I raise an eyebrow. "Did I miss it?"

A deep V mars his brows. "Woman, how often must I ask you to marry me? You know what? We're getting married. How's that?"

"You need to propose with a ring? And down on one knee? And have it videotaped, and maybe we can do an engagement photo shoot and party." I can hear the whiney sound of my voice, but I can't help it.

"Anything else?" he asks, grabbing my carry-on and wheeling it behind us as we head to the car park.

"I borrowed Alex's car to pick you up."

"The low rider? Ugh!"

Keston drops the bag and picks me up in his arms. "Is the pavement too hot for your princess's toes? Is the sun too bright for your delicate eyes? Are my kisses too intense for your damn lips?"

He presses his lips down on mine and sucks all the life force out of me with a tongue that won't quit.

I relax in his arms like a cat. "You know how to get me to shut up, don't you," I grumble.

"That's my job."

I struggle to get out of his arms, but he squeezes me tight.

"You're not going anywhere until you tell me you missed me, love me, and can't wait to scream my name to the sky. Or else?"

"Or else what?" I dare him.

The twinkle in his eyes darkens. "You really want to find out here?"

I shudder. "No. I know how you are."

He drops my feet to the ground unceremoniously. "Let's make it to the car."

"Not in Alex's car!"

"It's what you get for complaining."

I eye him sideways. The thing about Keston Kips is that he surprises me every day. When I think I have him wrapped around my finger, he shows me I am a fool, even to think I have that kind of control over him.

Keston glances at his watch as we reach the heavily tinted purple low rider that barely rolls over the potholes in St. Nicholas's roads.

"We have twenty minutes before I have to return to work. Let's make it good."

"Wait. What?"

He hustles my wheelie into the trunk, slides my butt inside the back seat, and rips off his tee shirt.

A huge grin lights up his face. "What're you waiting on, missy? It's been one week!"

"Keston, it's broad daylight."

"No one can see inside here."

"It's hot."

He leans over the driver's seat, inserts the keys, and starts up the car, spinning the A/C knob to the highest level.

"It's about to get a lot hotter." He smirks.

I shove my purse into the front seat. "Kes, I was just making a promise to myself."

He slides my panties down my legs.

Why do I wear these sundresses when I know he's uncontrollable? Am I a collaborator?

"What's your promise?" he whispers, sliding his calloused hands up and down my legs as if getting reacquainted with my body.

He presses light kisses on the inside of my thighs, and I inhale sharply.

"I want to remember all my sexual encounters, the who, what, when, where, and why."

"You only need to remember my name. So the who is done."

I smile for the first time after the long trip. "True."

"Now lie back and close your eyes. Let me give you something you'll never forget."

I giggle. "You promise?"

"I can do more than a promise," he says, sliding a long, thick finger between my legs.

At the touch of his hand on my clit, my hips buck upwards right where he wanted them in the first place.

He grins like a mad scientist and dives under my flimsy cotton dress. "Now we're talking," he says.

"Oh my God," I cry. I always forget how masterful he is with his tongue and hands. His fingers play me like a piano.

His tongue does not let up as it laps at my clit and my pussy, sopping up every bit of my juice flowing down my legs.

"You're a monster," I whisper.

"The one and only," he laughs.

I close my eyes and let myself fall off the edge of reality and into pure bliss.

All I hear is his mouth sucking on my pussy. All I feel are his fingers sliding in and out of my honeypot.

My hips jerk up and down mercilessly as I grab Keston's curly hair in my hands.

"Don't stop," I beg breathlessly.

He swishes his head from side to side, his nose rubbing against my clit on purpose.

This man takes sex to a whole new level, using every bit of himself on me until I am a drenched paper doll.

"You missed me?" he asks, tonguing circles around my clit, but never touching it.

"Yes," I shout, not caring if anyone is around. "I missed you so much."

"That's more like it." And with those words, he ramps up his speed — tongue, fingers, tongue, fingers until I am a hot mess, my legs windmilling over his head.

"I'm coming," I scream.

Keston does not stop as promised. He rolls his tongue exquisitely across my entire pussy, until I'm shaking so hard I lose all control.

In one momentous push of his fingers inside my pussy I

grab his head and scream his name. Ripples of pure heaven roll down my spine.

I'm crying and begging all at the same time.

My clit quivers under his firm lips.

When I've finished shaking, he raises a triumphant face.

"Welcome home, CJ."

I throw both arms wide, stretch my legs, and let my head loll to the side. "You win. I'll stop complaining."

"Ah, baby, don't do that. I love your complaints." He winks.

I smack his arm. "You're a sadist."

He frowns. "I don't know what that means. But if it means you'll scream my name, then yes."

"I feel sorry for Alex. He can't ever know what happened in the back seat of his precious car."

Keston glances at his watch. He jumps out of the car and opens the trunk. He returns waving a mini vac in one hand and a spray bottle in the other.

"Move your butt, we got work to do."

I roll my eyes.

"Don't tempt me; there's more." Keston points to the bulge in his pants.

"Ohhh! I love more."

I never get to find out what "more" there is because my phone rings loudly.

I grab it as it lights up on the car seat.

"It's Lucy," I say excitedly to Keston.

I am smiling like a mad woman, delighted my daughter is reaching out to me so soon. It's only been three days since we saw each other.

"Guess what?" she says, her voice rising in excitement.

"What?" I ask happily.

"I found him."

The smile of joy disappears.

"Him?" My heart hammers in my chest cavity. I leap out of the back seat of the car and start pacing.

Keston stops and stares. "You okay?"

I hold up one finger. "One second."

"Maybe you should sit down," Lucy says, her voice losing its excitement and filling with concern. "Are you sure you want to know?"

I press a hand to my head. "Do I?" I ask myself.

But Lucy's enthusiasm tells me she wants to share this with me. No matter who it is, I need to be there for her.

"Yes, I'm ready."

I'm hoping I recognize the man's name. And not draw a blank when she announces it.

She clears her throat. We're on an audio call, but I imagine her face with its freckles, dark curls, and pointed chin—the most beautiful face.

"Do you know a man named Marcus O'Brien? I'm almost sure he's my biological father."

The phone tumbles out of my hand.

"CJ!" Keston shouts, rushing to grab me as I sink down, knees buckling, head swimming with the news.

"What's the matter, baby?"

He grabs my phone off the ground and says, "I'm sorry. CJ is not well. Can she call you back?"

Even from a distance, I can hear Lucy ask worriedly, "Is she all right? Is Marcus O'Brien the right man?"

Keston holds the phone away from his face. He looks at me.

"The right man for what?"

Chapter Eight

The kite-flying competition is the talk of the town.

As Keston drives slowly through Skye Harbor, stopping for tourists wandering around, their eyes on the colorful fruits and wares for sale, I read the banners pasted on every conceivable surface.

On lamposts, sides of buildings, and even on banners on the promenade, they are fluttering in the breeze.

The victor will be crowned the King (or Queen) of St. Nicholas Day, a title that comes with a crown and a prize.

Probably a bottle of rum like at the Pirate Regatta.

I'm glad I returned in time to watch Keston fly one of his beauties. Even if the atmosphere in Alex's car is as chilly as the winter solstice right now.

"Are you going to tell me what's going on?" His lips are pulled in. His voice has deepened to a dangerously low pitch.

"I have to find out more information." I stall.

"More information about your ex-boyfriend? I thought he was out of our lives for good."

I put my hand on Keston's leg to soothe any raw feelings he still harbors for the man who kept us apart on purpose.

Marcus did Keston a big favor, sure, but he also did it to control a situation. He had no right to manipulate me and Keston the way he had.

It's no wonder Keston lacks *any* goodwill toward the billionaire Marcus O'Brien.

"I need to talk to Lucy," I say, turning the A/C high. "I don't know anything for sure right now. Can you give me that chance, please?"

Keston presses his lips even more tightly together.

He nods and stares out the window.

"Thanks."

Good grief, what the hell have I done now? My thoughts race back to twenty years ago.

If what Lucy is saying is correct, my life just got a whole lot more complicated.

And just when I thought I was settling down and ready to live a life of love and happiness with the man of my dreams.

The past has a way of sneaking forward to haunt or destroy you.

Keston drops me off and says he's taking the car to Alex and then returning to work.

"You'll be okay here until I return later?"

"Yes, of course." I put on a cheery smile to ease his worry. I miss his smiling, happy face.

"Everything will be fine, Kes," I say, tiptoeing and kissing his cheek. Behind my back, I have two fingers crossed.

"Will it?" he murmurs.

"Yes," I say as confidently as I can. "I'll make it okay."

He leaves without planting a kiss on my head, as usual. I feel awful. I don't think he did it on purpose.

Keston doesn't have a mean bone in his body. At least not toward me. To Marcus, that may be a different story.

I hustle inside and change my clothes. I throw on shorts and a tank and head outside to find Trixie, my donkey.

First things first.

Like most relationships, Trixie and I did not begin as bosom buddies. We worked our way slowly, from enemies to friends to besties.

The grey and white, large-eyed donkey and I are now inseparable.

"Hey, Trixie," I call as I wander the beach, sinking my bare toes into the cool, dark sand.

There's nothing better than the feel of the warm blue sea cascading over my feet as I stroll along, picking up seashells and pretty stones from the shore.

"*Hee Haw!*" Trixie trots up behind me, her tail whisking with joy.

At least, I assume it's joy. I fling my arms around her neck and kiss her nose.

She shimmies and shakes her large head.

I slip a carrot out of my shorts' pocket and feed it to her.

"Have you been a good girl?" I ask, rubbing the mohawk-style hair that trails down her neck.

Her head bobs up and down.

"I'll take that as a yes, unlike yours truly, who is causing all kinds of mayhem."

Trixie's ears flicker in sympathy.

"Even Kes seems upset with me, and he's chill about everything."

Trixie drops her head and gazes at me with her large, dark eyes.

"You're on my side, though, right?"

"Hee-haw," she brays, scraping her hooves in the sand.

"Good girl."

We walk down the beach side by side until we reach the sharp, pointy rocks that separate Keston's land from whatever grows on the other side.

My hand nestles in Trixie's mane. Every once in a while,

she nuzzles her nose in my side as if to say, "I'm glad you're back."

"I missed you, too," I tell her. "Just don't start stealing my clothes off the line again."

It took me a long time to teach Trixie to ignore the pretty sundresses, jeans, and sun hats drying in the sunshine. I hope she hasn't forgotten while I was away.

On our way back to the wooden cottage, I notice the peeling blue shutters have been repainted while I was gone.

The wooden shutters are a bright sky blue. They stand out against the green trees and white sand surrounding the small home.

The deck looks shiny and varnished, too. My sweetheart was busy while I was away for the week.

Too bad I didn't notice all the changes when he dropped me off. I was too busy doing damage control over this Marcus situation.

I don't know what I'll do if it's true. I don't know what it'll mean to my life—and Keston's. Having a daughter is one thing.

Having a daughter whose father is a billionaire ex-boyfriend who blackmailed Keston to stay away from me is another.

My heart clenches at the idea of losing Keston. He's the best man I've ever met.

He may not have the money or opportunities as the guys I have dated, but he's got something better; he adores me and supports me in following my dream.

"Once I figure out what my dream is, Trix," I stroke the donkey's fur.

Trixie has led me to the river that flows from the rainforest to the sea.

She stops to drink the clear, cool water.

I splash my bare feet in the water, washing off the sand.

"Trixie, look." I point to two hammocks strung up in the shade of the coconut trees. One is placed close to a tree stump so I can climb in and out of it and use the stump as leverage to push myself.

Tears prick my eyes. "Please, God, don't let me lose this man."

I wish I could climb in, sleep, and forget about Marcus O'Brien, my ex-boyfriend of five years before I met Keston.

But Marcus's story and mine didn't *begin* five years ago.

Something I've never told anyone.

Chapter Nine

"What the hell, CJ?" Giselle, my best friend, screeches.

We're on a group video chat. After returning to the house with Trixie, I waited as long as I could.

I unpacked, made a sandwich, sat on the porch staring at the waves breaking on the shore, then caved.

My friend group and I have been through a lot together over twenty years since meeting at Howard University. But lately, secrets have been tumbling out of our closets like skeletons at a frat party.

"What's one more life-changing event?" I grumble at the way Giselle stares at me, her perfect eyebrows hitting her hairline.

"I thought you shared your big secret with us already. Now this?" Giselle sighs. As a middle school principal, she's hardly ever rattled. But she looks shaken up now.

"I'm sorry," I say. "I don't even know if it's true. I'm waiting to talk to Lucy after her classes."

Katana sips from a cup. She chain drinks coffee to stay awake with her two babies. "*Another* plot twist! I swear CJ, your life is better than watching a Shonda Rimes series."

"I don't want it to be. I just want to settle down with Keston Kips and Trixie and live happily ever after."

"As you deserve to," chimes in Mikah, our supermodel friend, who visited me last month and fell in love with Keston's brother Kelley.

"Exactly," I mutter.

Lisa, our brilliant astrophysicist friend, joins the call, and Giselle fills her in.

"CJ got a call from Lucy."

Lisa's face lights up on my phone screen. Although it could be her lingering newlywed glow.

"How is Lucy doing?" Lisa asks, unwrapping a sandwich.

No one answers.

"Wait . . . why are you all looking sketchy? What's happening? What did I miss?"

"Marcus O'Brien might be CJ's baby daddy?" Giselle blurts without warning.

Lisa drops her sandwich. "What the fuck?"

We give a collective gasp. Lisa is the most wholesome of us. She doesn't curse or drink, has never smoked, and just married her college sweetheart.

As far as we know, her only vice is being friends with us.

My entire body heats up. And not from the sun shining across the tops of my feet perched on the railing. Admitting that Marcus may be Lucy's father is more embarrassing than not knowing who the father was.

"What Giselle means to say," I explain, "is that Lucy believes that based on her Ancestry results, Marcus O'Brien is . . . .um . . . *could* be her biological father."

"Hmmm," Katana says. "Sounds like you have some explaining to do. And not just to Lucy."

"Right. Marcus needs to know," Giselle nods vigorously.

"And Keston," adds Mikah.

"I know," I say sadly. "I hope Keston can deal with this."

"Am I missing something?" asks Lisa. "How is this possible? CJ met Marcus in an elevator at her law firm five years ago. They went out three times and fell in love."

"So we thought," Giselle growls. "You want to fill her in on the rest, CJ?"

I nod miserably. "Marcus and I met at Howard's alumni Homecoming weekend. Twenty years ago. When we started our Junior year, he was a returning alumnus. *Before* he moved to San Francisco and got rich."

"Oh." Lisa taps a finger on her lips. "I remember that weekend. We couldn't find you for two days."

Katana holds up three fingers.

Mikah laughs. "Let's say our girl was having a delicious time."

I cover my ears. "You're so mean."

"Why didn't you tell us you met Marcus years ago? What's the big deal?" Giselle leans back in her car seat. She takes all our video chats in the teachers' parking lot in her car.

"I don't think CJ remembered him?" Mikah says. "Did you, sweetheart?"

"Honestly, Homecoming weekend was always a blur," Katana says loyally. "I hardly recall who I danced with. Or kissed. Although I remember every penis I encountered."

They all eye me like I'm an alien species.

"Do you think an almost billionaire would ask me out just like that?" I snap my fingers. "He had his choice of women. Obviously, there was more to it."

"So, what really happened when you and Marcus ran into each other in that elevator five years ago?" Katana asks. "Because I've always imagined it was like a *Pretty Woman* scenario."

"CJ isn't a prostitute!" Giselle shrills.

"As far as we know," adds Lisa darkly. "She's got more secrets than the government."

I frown. "He said he wanted to go out with me because I liked him before he got rich. And he was looking for a strong, educated Black woman."

"Two out of three ain't bad," Giselle says.

Everyone hoots with laughter except me.

Tears threaten to fall. "I thought I'd get more support from you'll."

"Give CJ a break. I have a secret, too." Mikah leaps into the fray.

I mouth a silent "Thank you" for taking the heat off me.

Katana holds up a hand. "Hold up. I need to peek in on the kids. And pop some popcorn. I didn't expect I'd be watching a whole movie."

"Handle your business, woman," Mikah says.

Chapter Ten

hile Katana is gone, Giselle apologizes, "I'm sorry, CJ. I love you, but I wonder if the feeling is mutual. How can you not tell your best friend such important details about your life?"

Lisa stirs her cup of yogurt after giving up on her sandwich. "It seems as if CJ buries her head in the sand when faced with anything unpleasant. Probably stems from a childhood event."

"I thought you were a space scientist. Not a psychologist," Mikah pouts. "You've been blessed with brains and *more* brains?"

I laugh with relief. Our friend group thrives on teasing each other. We've been through Lisa's cancer scare, Katana's loss of both parents followed by her quick marriage, and Giselle's constant search for the "right" school to head up.

And, of course, my own misadventure and near-death when I was stranded with Keston on No Man's Land.

We can get through anything together.

Katana returns, a bag of popcorn in one hand and her newest little one tucked under her other arm.

The four of us break into wide smiles.

"Show us the cutie," Lisa purrs.

Katana waves away her request.

"I'm breastfeeding; just keep talking. Where were we? Oh yeah, Mikah was about to give us some juicy dirt."

Katana eyes Mikah with a gleam in her eye. "Finally."

Wait, what finally?" asks Giselle.

"Yeah, what?" Lisa echoes her.

I don't say a word because I think I know what Miakh is about to share. I discovered her huge secret when she was visiting St. Nicholas Island last month.

"Yes, Mikah, why don't you tell us all your secrets." I wink.

Mikah is like a cat playing with a toy mouse. She cocks

her head, swishes back her long hair, twirls her necklace around her neck, and sighs.

"Fine."

She drones in a boring monotone voice, "I'm not a supermodel. I'm an undercover spy."

Giselle gasps.

Lisa drops her yogurt cup and has to grab napkins to clean the mess. "What the hell are you talking about? I've seen you on magazine covers."

"Why don't Katana and CJ look surprised?" Giselle asks.

Mikah shrugs her slender shoulders. Even propped up in a bed at whatever hour it is in France, Mikah gives off supermodel energy.

"I'm a spy disguised as a supermodel," she explains. "Or vice versa."

"A what disguised as a who?" Giselle squeaks.

I'd laugh out loud if this shit weren't as sketchy as some of the stuff I've hidden.

"I think Mikah is saying she hustles between two jobs," I say.

"Exactly." Mikah smiles at me. "Thanks, CJ."

Now that the spotlight is off of me, I can relax and enjoy this unveiling.

"I can't talk about it," Mikah adds. "And neither can you. Unless you want to compromise my identity."

"Or get her killed," Katana says ominously.

Lisa makes the sign of the cross on her chest and kisses her fingers to the sky.

"I promise never to breathe a word. But can you tell us

about it? Who do you spy for? Are you a patriot or a traitor? Wait, don't tell me. I don't want to know."

We wait patiently for Lisa to finish rambling or thinking out loud, as she calls it.

"She's done," I whisper.

A long sigh comes from Mikah's phone.

"I'm only telling you now because I want to retire. Twenty years is a long time to do two jobs. And I may have a good reason to retire," she smiles.

Something Mikah rarely does. Probably from all those years of pouting on the runway.

"Are you, by chance, referring to Kelley Kips?" I ask sweetly.

When Mikah visited me in St. Nickolas for one week to ensure I was okay, she met Keston's brother Kelley.

It was love at first sight for Mikah. I still haven't gotten Kelley's side of the story.

"He has something to do with it," she says cryptically,

I secretly cheer. I'd give anything for one of my besties to join me here on St. Nicholas Island. Think of the happy hours we could spend at the Cocoa Reef Resort.

"Can we get back to the news that Mikah is a . . . um . . .?" Giselle, who is not usually at a loss for words, looks seriously confused.

Lisa waves a hand high. "Yes, please, are you in any danger? Are *we* in any danger for knowing you?"

Four of us stare blankly at the screen. Katana hugs her baby closer.

Before Mikah can answer that, I say in a hush-hush voice, "Do you carry a weapon?"

Mikah snorts, "*pons.*"

"What does that mean?

Giselle interprets. "I think that's the plural for a weapon. Am I right?"

Mikah yawns. "Yes, yes. I carry what I need to carry when it's appropriate. But not usually. History has revealed other models who were also spies, so I'm not the first."

Giselle swivels around as if checking over her shoulder. "I think you need to retire as soon as possible."

Mikah stretches like a cat, her slim arms reaching for the ceiling. I wish I had that same carefree attitude to life.

"I'll keep you posted. Meanwhile, let's give CJ a break on the Marcus baby daddy scenario."

"I can see why she's a good spy," mutters Lisa. "Look at how she distracted us."

Mikah grins. "What will I do with my life once I retire at forty? I don't have any transferrable skills to the modern-day workforce."

"I'll think of something for you," Katana says.

"What about for me?" I beg. "I need to find a new career on this tiny island."

They all look at me stumped. "What does Keston suggest?' asks Giselle.

"He says I should wait until I find what I love doing. Something that makes me happy."

"That man adores you," says Mikah. "You better not fuck it up. For yourself or for me. I'm still figuring out things with Kelley."

I can't imagine any man not doing whatever Mikah

wants. But it seems Kelley has a mind of his own and is not easily swayed by her beauty or charm.

Probably because he's as beautiful, if not more so, than Mikah.

Giselle clears her throat. "I have to return to my life as a principal. The most exciting thing that happened to me was when a fifth grader proposed to me in the hallway."

"Awwww," we all say together, then laugh.

"Did you let him down easily?" Katana asks.

"Who said it was a him?" Giselle snaps. "You guys make fun of me while you travel the globe, meet exciting men, and fall in love. Meanwhile, I'll continue to be responsible."

"Someone has to," Mikah says, giving us all the peace sign. "Now, can I go to sleep, my beauties? It's late here."

"Where's here?" asks Giselle. "Are you in Paris? Or some other part of France?"

Mikah puts a finger to her lips.

After Mikah hangs up, I turn to the rest of my friends. "Okay, guys, what do I do about Marcus?"

Katana sucks her teeth. "Write him an email. He deserves to know. But he doesn't need to ruin your life. Or Lucy's."

I frown. "He wouldn't do that."

"Are we talking about the same Marcus O'Brien who wanted to keep you and Keston apart? Who knows what he'll try after you tell him you are biological parents to Lucy?"

"Get all the facts first," Lisa adds.

I stare at a new email from Lucy, which came in during our chat. I have an ominous feeling that all the details are contained there.

"Don't get emotional in your email. Don't feel as if you owe him anything," Giselle says in a voice of reason.

"Your mental health comes first," Katana says. "Do what's best for you and your current relationship."

"Got it," I say. "Facts, email, no emotion, mental health, Keston."

"And congratulations, CJ. It looks like your dream of having Marcus's baby came true." Giselle smirks.

I smack my head with one hand. "Shut up! That was before I met Keston."

I throw kisses at my friends before hanging up.

Afterward, I swing in the porch swing, legs tucked under me, and contemplate Lucy's email.

I was right; it gives the data on her being Marcus's child.

"Well, Trixie," I address my cute donkey, snoring through my video call. "It looks as if we have some explaining to do."

Trixie lets out a fart.

"Ewww! You're disgusting."

She opens one eyelid and glares at me as if to say, "You should talk."

"True," I mutter.

My phone shows it's almost five. The sun will be sliding into the sea. The sky is already turning orangey pink.

Keston will be home soon. Hopefully, he can whip up a delicious cocktail for me—one with a lot of rum. I'm going to need it.

Chapter Eleven

Keston's rusty motorbike growls up to the house. I'm both excited and nervous to see him.

When he left, his forehead was all frowns. His lips were tight. His words were few.

Now, he may be more so after what I'm about to tell him.

Trixie runs down the steps at the loud banging.

Great. My only friend here has deserted me.

But I didn't need to worry. Keston Kips doesn't let much get him down.

"Hey, baby," he says, leaping off the bike and taking the front steps in one long vault.

Planting kisses all over my face, he nuzzles into my hair. "I missed you."

The tightness in my chest decreases. I can't give up this man. I won't give him up. I'll fight for us.

"I love you so much, sweetheart," I say.

He leans back, his gaze intense. He grasps my hands firmly. "Tell me."

I blanch.

"You never tell me that you love me so much. It's always, 'get away from me. Or stop, you're too clingy.'"

"Do I?"

"Yes, and then I punish you for being an ungrateful wrench."

"Oh," I smile a little. "Is that our routine?"

He nods vigorously. "And don't change it," he says, tickling my sides.

I yelp. "Stop."

"Never." To prove his point, he raises me onto his lap and tickles me while holding me down with one arm.

I almost do a Trixie fart.

For the next five minutes, I'm too busy squealing for help, shouting for him to release me, pounding my fists on his chest, and laughing my head off to remember I have sobering news to share.

Keston ends his tickling session by kissing my neck. Then, he dumps me back on the porch swing and heads inside.

"Hey, I have to tell you something," I mutter at his retreating back. Not loud enough for him to hear me.

I tried!

"I'm going to change and grab Megatron," he shouts.

"What? Who's Megatron?"

"My kite."

"It has a name?"

"Of course. By the way, you still haven't named our boat."

I tap my hands on the swing. "I will," I shout.

Since we returned barely alive from our last adventure, I haven't stepped foot into the boat. I'm not sure when I'll do it again, either.

My body shudders at the memory of the giant eel I came face to face with.

It's incredible how fast Keston recovered physically and emotionally from that encounter.

Maybe he'll do the same when I break my news to him.

I sigh as I gather my pile of curls into a messy bun. It's not as if it can kill him! He's a survivor. We both are.

We will deal with this just like we dealt with hurricane-force winds and a sea monster.

What's one disgruntled billionaire compared to those things?

"Are you talking to yourself again?" Keston asks.

He's stepped out of the house in a fresh pair of shorts and a tank top that reveals his rippling muscles.

I inhale sharply. He takes my breath away. Literally.

"No," I roll my eyes. But then I see the gigantic kite he's maneuvering through the doorway.

It's as tall as he is. And it's stunning, with different shades of blue in diamond patterns all over the larger-than-life bamboo frame. Small silver triangles pick up the setting sun and shine like natural diamonds.

"Whoa!" I exclaim. "That is . . . the most spectacular kite I've seen in my life."

He beams like he won a million-dollar quiz show.

"I mean it, Kes. I can't believe you built this while I was away. Where are we going to put this huge kite? It can be a statement piece in our home." I rub my hands together in excitement.

His beaming smile vanishes. "I'm flying Megatron. Don't get attached to it."

"Nooooo!" I squeal. "It's too beautiful. It's a work of art. You're going to lose it in the sea. It'll break, or the wind will take it away."

He nods. "All definite possibilities."

My face falls. "You have no idea how special that is, do you?"

A big grin lights up his eyes. "As special as you."

I groan. "There he is, ladies and gentlemen, my corny boyfriend."

"You mean *horny*, don't you?" He winks.

I suck my teeth. "I told you to build an ugly kite. What do you do? You make the most beautiful kite in the world."

"Let's go fly it. I have to test it out before the competition."

I squish up my mouth. I want to tell him about Marcus, but how can I when he looks so happy?

"Fine," I grumble. "But I'm not happy about this.

Chapter Twelve

The next hour is one of the craziest of my life. And I've done a lot of ridiculous things with this man already.

First, we walked all the way to a place called Cemetery Hill.

We can't take his motorbike because of the gigantic kite.

Then, we have to trudge up the winding hillside, passing gravestones to the left and right of the path.

"Don't step on any dead people," Kes says as I huff and puff behind him.

"I'll try not to," I say, walking as closely as possible in his footsteps. "There must be a better place to fly your kite than on top of your ancestors."

"Nope, Cemetery Hill has the best wind. They don't mind. We always fly our kites up here."

"Great. I see this will be a regular thing in our lives." I silently apologize to the buried Campbells and the Bruces, the Kips and the Walkers whose grave markers I pass along the way.

Keston's calf muscles ripple with each step. I can see where he got them. Trudging up and down this hill is a workout.

"I never brought a girl up here before. You're the first."

"Not even Tabitha?" I ask. She's Keston's ex-girlfriend, who hated me at first, but after our adventure with the giant eel, she tolerates me.

He looks over his shoulder. "I didn't bring her because she was flying her own kites here."

"Oh."

Once we arrive at the top of the hill and I catch my breath, I gaze around in amazement. There's a lot of wind, for sure. But the view is out of this world.

"We can see all the way to No Man's Land, Kes. Look!"

I can see in every direction. The blue shimmering ocean. The green hills of St. Nicholas. The colorful houses, like dots of candy on the hillsides. And the tiny islands offshore look like Xs and O's doting the landscape.

"Wow!"

Keston lays his kite gently on the ground and comes over to my side. "It is the best place to see everything."

"Like the top of the Empire State Building."

"But without Godzilla."

I giggle. "You're weird."

"And you're perfect." He kisses the top of my head.

That wipes the smile right off my face. I have to tell him now. I can't keep it in any longer.

Seeing No Man's Land right there brings back memories of being stranded on the island together.

Keston was the first person I told about giving birth to a daughter. He was the one who convinced me to share my secret. To not be afraid.

He loves me for me. And this is part of me, so he'll still love me.

I don't realize he's staring at me until I raise my face to his.

The look in his brown eyes is pure love.

He takes my chin in one hand and says, "You can tell me anything, CJ. I will always love you. Love is not a vase that breaks when it falls. It's a rubber band that you can stretch forever. It's a kite that you fly without fear of it falling. Even if it falls, you can find it. You can fix it. Or rebuild it brand new."

His words bring tears to my eyes. His unwavering belief in our love is a powerful medicine that heals my wounds. It gives me the courage to speak. I take a deep breath.

"I found out from Lucy. She confirmed that Marcus is most likely her biological father."

Keston blinks.

"I don't know how he'll take it. But Lucy wants me to tell him. She'd like to meet him. She's a bit stunned. Because of who he is."

Keston holds my hands. "How long have you and Marcus been together?"

"Five years. But I met him once a long time ago."

Keston nods. "Are you considering going back to him now that you're parents to Lucy?"

I inhale sharply. "That is not an option."

"Okay, that's all I wanted to know."

"I'm with you, Keston. I love you." The tears I was holding back fall on my cheeks. Or maybe it's the wind blowing in my eyes.

Either way, I find myself crying.

He covers me with both arms and rocks my shoulders. "You're safe with me, baby. Nothing is coming between us. I've waited too long to find you."

"Same," I sniffle. "I've waited longer than you."

"Right. Because you're the cougar."

I step back and dry my tears. "Don't make me hurt you. Say you're sorry."

He doesn't look sorry.

He holds up both hands. "What can I say, I'm your boy toy."

I smack him hard.

"Ouch, woman. That's abuse."

"I haven't even started," I say. "Now, let's fly that kite

before it gets totally dark up here, and I've got to walk down amongst your ghost relatives."

He laughs. "About that."

"What?"

"Well . . ., we have jumbies, not ghosts."

"What the hell's a jumbie?"

Keston carefully picks up his kite and shows me how to help him tie on the tail.

"They're kind of like ghosts. But . . . ."

"But what?"

He chuckles. "You'll see. Or hear."

"I don't want to see . . . or hear any jumbies."

"Shhh, you'll make them mad."

"Oh my God, are you for real? You brought me to a haunted hill."

He shrugs. Then, he launches his giant kite into the wind. It billows its mighty kite body up and down, dipping and diving like the villain robot it's named after.

"It's *their* hill. We're the visitors," he says. His face is lit up with the excitement of watching his giant kite rise higher and higher as it rides on the wind.

I stare at my boyfriend. Moments ago, I thought I loved him with every fiber of my being. Now, I want to push him off the hill. Him *and* his Megatron kite.

I swear love makes you crazy.

Chapter Thirteen

W atching the sunset from the top of Cemetery Hill may be worth whatever we encounter on our way back down.

I wish we'd brought a cooler of wine and snacks.

I sit on the short, clipped grass, sticking my legs out and leaning backwards on my hands.

It's relaxing watching Keston's kite hum in the faraway sky.

Until it soars out over the ocean. Then I hold my breath, hoping it doesn't fall out of the sky when the wind dies.

If anything, the breeze is so powerful that the kite could take Keston with it into the stratosphere.

"Hold on, honey," I shout encouragingly. "You got it."

From up here, the setting sun is an orange ball on a ribbon of sherbert colors.

An artist would love to capture its glory. I have only my phone camera, but I'm snapping photos like crazy.

Sitting outside, enjoying the feel of the grass between my toes, inhaling the sweet, fragrant air, and watching the sun kiss the sea goodnight, it's hard to believe it's the first week of December.

Now that I am a resident of St. Nicholas, I look forward to evenings like this one.

All my worries that I wouldn't be able to adjust to island life are disappearing. How could I not love this place?

Or the man flying the giant bird in the sky.

"So, we get two big holidays in December—St. Nicholas Day *and* Christmas?" I'm fighting to see in the dark, so I don't accidentally step on anyone's grave.

Keston and I are making our way back down Cemetery Hill after he safely reeled in his kite from the dark sky.

I'd watched silently as he wrapped up the tail and string. He declared it the one.

"My baby!" He said, kissing his kite.

I almost got jealous.

"I feel as if I have to clarify that Christmas will happen. I've invited Mikah, my mom, and Lucy."

"I finally get to meet your family," he says, walking ahead and hugging his kite close.

"Lucy isn't sure. I told her I'd make all the arrangements, like buying her a ticket and booking a room at the Cocoa Reef Resort. However, I think she'll spend the college break with her adopted family since she spent Thanksgiving with me and Mom."

"What about your mother?"

"Mom loves her old-fashioned, snowy, cold Christmas. It's a maybe from her. But Mikah is definitely coming."

"To see us or to see Kelley?" he laughs.

"Both. But definitely Kelley. I hope they'll become a couple. I'd be very happy if she moved or at least spent a lot of time here."

"I'll talk to Kelley."

"You can't make people fall in love, Kes. It has to happen organically. Like us."

"I don't know what you mean by *organically*. Either you fall in love, or you don't."

He reaches back to hold my hand as we step over some rocks.

"Maybe we can drop them off at No Man's Land and leave them there," he chuckles. "It worked for us."

At that moment, two things happen.

I'm hit with a flash of inspiration.

And I slip from the pathway.

I scream as my butt hits the ground.

"CJ!" Keston leaps to grab me, but it's too late.

I roll sideways down the slight incline right onto a mound of dirt.

Under the moonlight, a white, raggedy cross stares back at me.

I scream louder. Birds flutter from their nests. Dogs bark loudly. In the distance, a whistle pierces the air.

The cross tilts forward and keels over on top of me.

I scamper backward to get from under it, but all I'm doing is messing up the grave more.

The cross is heavy—an old-fashioned wooden one that weighs a ton.

"Keston," I whimper.

He drops his kite and skates downward, avoiding the grave.

He spreads his legs wide and reaches over to yank me up without touching the dirt.

"It's okay, baby. Just apologize."

"To the grave?"

"Yes. We don't play around with jumbies. They can ruin your life. Then we'd have to go to an obeah woman for her to create a spell to fix it."

I stare at him in the dark. "Seriously?"

"Yup. Jumbies are no joke here."

I turn to the grave before I dust off my clothes. "I'm sorry."

Keston lugs the wooden cross upwards and tries to stick it back in its foundation, but it topples back over.

"Oh, oh," he says. "We'll have to leave it and get help tomorrow."

"I've ruined his or her grave," I cry. "Is the jumbie going to come get me?"

Keston doesn't respond.

I shine my phone light on the cross. "At least let me see whose grave I desecrated."

I read aloud, "*Gang Gang Sarah.*"

What kind of name is that?

I continue, "Born in Africa unknown, died December 6, 1880. Look, Kes, she died on St. Nicholas Day."

"Fuck," Keston says. "The witch of Golden Trace. Let's get out of here."

All the blood rushes from my body. My knees weaken. Have I ruined the grave of an African witch? Who was in a gang? A *gang gang*?

I whimper as I scuttle down behind Keston. I've never seen him move so fast.

"CJ," he says softly, "Remember when I said nothing can come between us?"

"Yes," I whisper.

"Well, this is the only thing that could."

"What do you mean?"

"If Gang Gang Sarah puts a spell on us, we're doomed."

Chapter Fourteen

W e walk the rest of the way down the hill in silence. The pathway of dirt and rocks looks perilous now that I know what can happen if I fall.

Arriving on the black asphalt roadway, I release the breath I've been holding.

"Thank God. I've never been so happy to see cement in my life."

Now that we're out of the hilly graveyard, I feel braver.

"I don't believe in jumbies. If you don't believe, they can't bother you."

Keston's hand claps over my mouth. He shakes his head. "Where did you hear that?" His eyes are large and round. Is he pranking me?

I'm not sure where I heard that. Or read it. Maybe from a Stephen King novel before the unsuspecting, non-believing family got murdered in their sleep.

I keep that information to myself.

"It's true," I bluster. "Ask anyone."

"Not anyone on St. Nicholas Island," he says spookily.

"Why'd we have to fly your kite on Cemetery Hill? Isn't that asking for trouble?"

Keston stares at me like I've lost my senses. Which I'm close to doing.

"No one has ever fallen on a grave before? As far as I know."

The sinking feeling in my stomach crashes to my toes. "Except me."

Megatron rustles in the breeze, reminding us to get moving. My legs are wobbly. I hope they will support me all the way home.

"Should I be scared? Is this like voodoo?" As we walk along the dark roadway, I stick close to Keston.

"Back home in upstate New York, we have many urban

legends about supernatural beings. Like Bigfoot and the Headless Horseman. But no one believes they're real today."

"It's different here. Our jumbies, soucouyany, ligahoo, and Papa Bois are part of our traditional culture. They live amongst us."

"That's a lot of stuff."

"That's just a few. We have mer folks who live in the sea."

"Mermaids?" I ask hopefully.

"No, we have mermen. You'd like them. Very handsome with long hair."

"Your mermen have dreadlocks?"

Keston's laugh makes me feel better. "I've never seen any. But fishermen who go out late at night to fish have."

"I think this is information I should have had before I moved to this island."

"Our folklore comes from West Africa. It's not just our island. The other Caribbean islands share similar creatures. Not the mermen, though. That's special to us."

"I'd like to meet a handsome merman," I muse aloud.

"You already have a man. A normal, two-legged one."

"I know that!"

A woman can dream, can't she?

"Stop thinking about how you can meet one."

"How do you know what I'm thinking?"

"Because you are smiling and looking dreamy and haven't complained about how long this walk is."

"True. Are we almost there? My legs hurt. You forget I'm older than you."

"How can I forget? You remind me whenever it's in your best interest."

We reach the gravelly turn off to Keston's land. Trixie is standing under the streetlamp waiting for us.

"Trixie," I cry out. "Save me."

Our adorable donkey trots over and nuzzles her head into my shoulder. "I missed you too, sweetie. We have a lot to talk about."

"Hee-haw," she brays.

Keston ruffles her mane. "Why don't you ride her the rest of the way."

I rub Trixie's long face. "I'm not riding her. She's our pet."

"A pet that can carry you and me and Megatron if we needed her to. Get your ass up on her back, woman."

I eye Trixie's swaying backside. My legs do hurt from falling on top of Gang Gang Sarah's grave.

"Trix, you okay with me riding you?"

As if she understands, she stops in the middle of the gravelly road.

"I'll take that as a yes. Now how do I do this?"

Kes rests his "baby" gently down on the side of the road. "She's short, just grab her mane and throw a leg over."

I edge up to Trixie's side. "You ready?"

Trixie shakes her head up and down. "This is one smart animal. I am impressed."

"Donkeys are highly intelligent. They learn quickly so you can teach her stuff. And they're smarter than horses."

"Wow, Trixie, you hear that?"

I rub her hair before grasping her mane and swinging one leg over her back.

At least, that was my intention. I swing too hard and end up sliding across her back instead.

Keston catches me before I fall. I feel as sexy as a pigeon trying to pole dance. He lifts me and plops me down in the center of Trixie's back.

"Spread your legs woman. Grip her sides."

I roll my eyes. "I *am* spreading my legs. This is as far as they go."

Keston snorts. "Not in my experience."

"You're lucky I'm up here, and you're down there."

He tiptoes and kisses my lips. "Enjoy the ride."

He taps Trixie on her butt and the donkey sways down the road. "What do I hold on to?" I shout.

Keston walks behind us with his kite. "Her neck. Or her mane, anything."

"I need reins."

"Nobody rides donkeys with reins."

Before I can retort, Trixie picks up her pace and leaves Keston behind.

I'm giggling and squealing. My hands hold onto Trixie's spiky mohawk. My butt jostles up and down.

It only takes me a few minutes to feel her rhythm, and then I go with the flow.

"Way to go, Trix," I compliment her.

"Hee-haw!" she brays into the night.

When she reaches the beach house, she stops by the front steps for me to slide off.

"You really are a smarty pants."

She shimmies to the side like she's dancing. I grab a few carrots from the fridge and feed them to her.

"Trixie, my dear, if you're so smart, you've got to stop Gang Gang Sarah from putting a bad spell on me and Keston. We've survived a lot already. A hurricane, a sea monster, and a pirate lair, we can't let a dead African witch destroy us."

Trixie nods her head in agreement.

"Do this for me, and I'll let you wear one of my sundresses."

Her hee-haw is as loud as thunder.

"Are you bribing our donkey?" Keston asks, walking up.

I have the nerve to look guilty.

"Maybe."

Chapter Fifteen

St. Nicholas Day arrives with clear blue skies. Nothing strange has happened to me yet!

I hope I've been spared because Keston went with friends to fix Gang Gang Sarah's gravestone the day after the Cemetery Hill incident.

I stayed at home.

I didn't mind because I was busy outlining my flash of inspiration. The one I had right as I tumbled down the hill onto the sacred grave.

I can't wait to discuss it with Keston after today.

He's been wrapped up with Megatron and building smaller kites to give to kids at the festival. He's hardly had time to seduce me in or outdoors per his usual.

Not that he lets me forget what's in store once St. Nicholas Day is done.

When I woke up this morning to find him gluing more kite paper to bamboo frames, he smiled and said, "After I win, I'm all yours, baby."

"What if you don't win?"

He scowled. "Don't jinx me, woman. We have enough bad ju ju riding against us."

"Right," I muttered. "Sorry."

And I was sorry. I don't want to release any negative energy for Gang Gang Sarah to latch onto. I'm surrounding myself with positivity and good vibes, hoping for the best.

"You'll win. Megatron is awesome."

"Now you're talking." He finishes another colorful kite.

This one has pink and yellow diamonds with a long pink tail. I wish it were for me. I wish all his kites were mine.

What a grinch you are, CJ. These are for the children.

Keston's generosity inspires an idea of my own.

"Hey, Kes, if this African witch is so special, she should have a better grave marker. Why don't we raise funds to fix her gravestone? That way, she'll forgive me."

He stopped what he was doing and stared out to sea.

"I don't think she'd want anything fancy. She was a healer who came from Africa to watch over her enslaved people. The colonists called her a witch. But she represented hope."

"Oh," I breathed. "I don't mean to discredit her."

I'm really going to get it now.

"I know you don't, sweetheart. Maybe think of ways to honor her spirit that don't directly benefit you. That's the heart and soul of St. Nicholas."

He smiled gently at me and wiped his brows.

"Sure," I muttered. "I'll Google ideas. How to appease an African deity."

Kes wasn't listening. I was so used to being the center of his attention that it felt strange not to have it.

But this happens in all relationships, I suppose. The honeymoon period wears off.

Or maybe . . . this was Gang Gang Sarah already working to destroy us.

As I shower and slip into a cute sundress to celebrate St. Nicholas Day, I think about what Keston said.

How can I pay my respects to Gang Gang Sarah's model of caring and hope? She sounds like a saint. No way I can live up to that.

Although Kes does.

He finishes gluing the last of about one hundred small kites and gives me a side-eye.

"I'm going to change my clothes. Do not touch these kites. They are for the kids. Not for on top of the fridge or dresser."

"I wasn't." I huff, although I had my eye on at least five beauties.

"I see you marking them."

He stuffs them carefully into a large garbage bag and ties the top. "There."

"Whoa, no faith, mister."

He kisses the top of my nose as he strolls by. "It pays to know your woman."

Ten minutes later, he returns in a red T-shirt and white linen pants. One that Kelley made from his homegrown hemp material.

Something about that linen material makes these Kip's men look hotter than usual. It accentuates their slim hips and their um . . . packages.

I eyeball my man and give him two thumbs up.

He grins and does a MJ spin.

"Wanna be starting something," he sings in a falsetto voice, twirling me around on the porch.

Trixie brays as if joining in.

With the blue sea shining just a few feet away and the sun playing peek-a-boo with the clouds, today is a good day to start something new.

"You ready, babe?" Kes picks up the garbage bag and swings it over one broad shoulder.

I cover my mouth to stop laughing.

"What?" he blinks.

"You look like a very hot Santa with that sack. All you're

missing is a Santa hat."

He preens. "Just call me Mr. Claus."

I lean on the porch railing as he tries to figure out how to carry the garbage bag on the back of his motorcycle.

"Can I sit on Santa's lap, please?"

"That's not going to work," he growls.

"What?" I ask.

"The bag. I made too many kites. I'm going to have to leave some home." He looks saddened.

"Can you call someone to pick them up in a car?"

He shakes his head. "All the guys are already headed to the field."

At that moment, Trixie wanders over. The little bell I tied around her neck tinkles with her steps.

I swear, she knows when she's needed.

Chapter Sixteen

It's clear to me what I must do. I must channel the spirit of Gang Gang Sarah and not think about myself. Hard as hell for a New Yorker to do.

We didn't get a reputation for being pushy for nothing. It really is a shove-or-be-shoved world there.

How you hold in your tummy to squeeze onto a crowded subway car.

Or pretend to be scrolling on your phone to look "distracted" when you're actually waiting to jump into the next taxi that stops to let out a passenger before anyone else can grab it.

Or brazenly sliding into a traffic lane without putting on your blinkers because if you do, no one will let you in.

I'm a dead-ass New Yorker and changing my natural me-first behavior will be hard.

But if it helps me keep this amazing man, adjust to this island mentality, and earn Gang Gang Sarah's sympathy, I'm going to do it.

Damn! Keston said I have to do these things without directly benefiting myself.

Arrrrgh!

"What's wrong? You look like you're wrestling with the devil on your shoulder."

"More like the angel."

He snorts. "What angel?"

I stop our bantering before it escalates to sex on the porch.

"I can carry the bag of kites on Trixie's back," I state firmly so I don't back out. "You can ride the motorbike and get there on time for the kite competition."

"*Whaaaat?*"

"You heard me."

Honestly, I doubt I can repeat it as confidently as I did the first time.

"No baby," Kes argues. "You look too cute in your dress

with your hair and makeup done. I can't let you ride the donkey five miles."

This may seem like a small moment. But it's huge. What I do and say now will pave the way for my future on St. Nicholas and with Keston Kips.

"Thank you." I square my shoulders. "But I insist."

The horrified look on his face confirms he's as shocked as I am.

"What have you done with my sweet, grouchy, complaining, heart-of-gold girlfriend?"

I suck my teeth. "Way to give me a compliment sandwich." I swish into the house. "I'll be right back."

I dig in my drawers for the pair of bike shorts I brought. I slip it on under my dress. So much for my lacy panties.

When I return, I clamber up on Trixie's back as if I do it every day instead of only once.

I fluff out my dress around my brown thighs. "Give me the bag."

Keston hands me the bag silently. His eyebrows are way up on his forehead. His lips look as if they don't know whether to smile or smirk.

"I swear, woman, you're always surprising me."

"I surprise myself," I mutter under my breath.

I click my heels against Trixie's sides like I've seen in the movies when the hero is about to ride off into the sunset.

Trixie nips my ankle like she's saying, "Easy there, mama."

"Sorry," I stroke her fur. "I was getting a bit carried away in the moment. Help me be impressive, nuh."

"Are you sure about this?" Kes asks for the tenth time.

"Let's stop wasting time; We have places to be."

Trixie hee-haws in agreement.

I swing the bag to my other hand. It's as light as a feather considering how much it contains.

The bamboo and tissue kites weigh nothing.

Keston strides across the yard to the clothesline. He uses his serrated blade he carries and cuts a piece of the line.

"What are you doing?"

His fingers fly as he braids the pieces into what looks like a pair of sturdy reins.

If I've learned anything from living on St. Nicholas it's that most everyone is a seasoned McGyver.

Kes ties the reins around Trixie's neck and hands the ends to me.

"For you to hold onto."

I grip the reins in one hand and the bag in the other. Trixie's slow pace means I can switch hands with no problem. "Thank you."

Keston kisses my lips.

"Who's the Santa now?" he chuckles. "The kids will be excited when you arrive with the kites."

I don't answer. I'm volunteering to be uncomfortable to help a situation. Not to be rewarded.

And it's all because of Gang Gang Sarah.

I may not believe in African deities, witches, or merfolks, but I believe in karma. And good karma means doing for others what you want them to do for you.

Keston snaps a few pics of me and Trixie before we head down the dirt road.

Then he leaps onto his cycle and rolls down the road carefully so as not to spook Trixie.

"Nothing scares you, though, right?" I tell my donkey as I sway and roll down the island's roads.

If only my New Yorker friends could see me now. This proves anyone can adapt, change, and improve.

Even me.

"Hee-haw!"

Chapter Seventeen

The festival is being held on a field outside Skye Harbor, St. Nicholas's main town. The road there is long, dusty, and lonely.

If only I could complain to somebody. I'm sweaty. I'm

dusty. My hand hurts from clutching the bag of kites. And I think I smell of Trixie's farts.

Not to mention, the hem of my dress is covered in red dust from the roadways.

Trixie takes her time, swiveling her head to check on me every few minutes until I pull the reins and keep her looking forward.

"Today, Trixie. We want to get there today."

But Trixie is a smell-the-roses donkey. Whenever we pass a tempting bush or plant, she can't resist and stops to stick her head into it.

We pass a garden of lime trees, and I inhale the sharp scent of citrus and the sweet scent of lavender.

"Don't eat the flowers," I warn.

I pull gently on the reins to point her in the right direction.

As we descend the last hill, I hear the shouts of children before I see them.

Kites zip and zap across the sky, sounding like mini airplanes. I look for Keston's Megatron. But I can't focus on the sky between holding on for dear life and steering around potholes.

The last thing I need is to fall into a hole.

"I already look terrible," I mutter to Trixie.

She swishes her tail.

"Yesh, yeah, you did your best to get me here. I appreciate it."

We pass another donkey on the road. It's pulling a cart full of coconuts. A weather-beaten man sits on the front of the cart. He has real reins that he snaps like a pro.

He must be on his way to sell his coconuts at the festival.

I wave as we pass by.

Trixie shakes her head at the male donkey and brays loudly. I almost fall off her back.

"Hey, warn a girl when you're going to flirt, please."

St. Nicholas Day is being celebrated on a football (soccer) field.

Streamers in the island's colors of blue and coral decorate the goalposts, the trees, and the food trucks lined up along one side of the grounds.

A breeze flutters the streamers and wafts the delicious curry and BBQ chicken scents my way.

"I hope there's food left for us, Trixie."

She snorts in agreement.

Children run helter-skelter across the field as parents and other grown-ups mingle in groups, drinks in their hands.

Elders are playing chess on makeshift tables with overturned buckets for seats.

A table on one end holds trophies for all the competitions. The flyers mentioned goat races, crab races, sack races, and all other kinds of races.

Another table is set up under a tent, where a DJ plays music. Teenagers stand around in front of the speakers, getting their eardrums busted.

Arriving on a donkey at this event should be no big deal. But it's very different from arriving in a regular old car.

When Trixie steps into the festival grounds with me on her back, we're greeted with clapping, piercing whistles, and shouts of, "She's here!"

Keston must have told them I'd be arriving with the kites.

The welcome is worth the past hour of sweaty, slow trudging over the hot roads.

"Trixie, we're famous," I pat her neck. "Don't worry I'll get you water and snacks as soon as I climb down from here."

All around the field, people are smiling and snapping pics of me, Trixie, and the giant bag of goodies I'm carrying over one shoulder.

I almost do a Kate Middleton wave. Except I have to grip the reins.

Children of all sizes run pell-mell at full speed toward us.

I don't want to end up in another viral video — this one would be titled, *"New Yorker tumbles off a donkey and squashes a child."*

"Don't get spooked, Trix. I got you."

But Trixie is anything but spooked. She does a little dance, lifting her feet one by one like a horse that won a Grand Prix race.

"Show off," I mutter. "Don't knock me over."

As if she heard me, Trixie slowly lays down in the grass.

I swing my legs to the side and slide off her back. "Ta-da!"

But no one cares. Trixie is the star of the show. She does a victory trot around the field to loud cheering.

Hmmm.

Keston saunters over, a big smile on his face. In one hand, he's holding a spool of thread attached to a kite high up in the sky.

"She's so cool," says a little boy.

"Me?" I gasp.

"I think he means Trixie," Keston says. "But you are cool, too. To me." He leans over to kiss my lips. His mouth is cool, firm, and just what I need after that ride.

I blush. "Thank you, sir."

Trixie returns to my side. I whisper in her ear. "Show off."

She shakes her head up and down.

"Own it, baby girl," I laugh.

"Can I pet her?" asks the same little boy.

"Me, too," shouts another child, followed by a chorus of, "No, me. Me!"

The raucous is unbelievable.

I assess the little beings. "Where's the sharing spirit of St. Nicholas Island? We can all take turns petting Trixie, but first, we must give her water. She's thirsty after her long walk."

Ten kids scamper off across the field. I hear them shouting, "I'll get her water."

Keston watches me with admiring eyes. "You sure are good with children."

"I have lots of practice with you."

"Ha!"

Do I know how to interact with kids, though? I don't have any experience. The memory of feeling like an imposter with Lucy shatters any notion that I could be good with kids.

Keston tugs on his kite thread. "It's okay to be nervous. "

"I'm not nervous."

He raises an eyebrow.

I'm fucking terrified. But I keep that to myself. One day, we'll have our own children and I won't know what to do.

Being a mother requires infinite patience and understanding. And something else . . . a suit of armor. How else can you survive watching your kid fall and hurt herself?

Like right now.

A little girl is carrying water in what appears to be the bottom half of a gallon water bottle that's been cut in two. She's hurrying on her short legs toward Trixie when she trips and falls.

The water goes flying. She looks at the empty makeshift jug and cries her little heart out.

My own heart clenches in distress.

I race over and pick her up. "It's okay, sweetie. We can get more water. Are you okay?"

She points at Trixie. "But she's thirsty."

Two boys race up, carrying a large bowl of water. "Momma says we have to bring back the bowl," the younger one announces.

I take the girl's hand.

We join the others stooping next to Trixie, who is calmly drinking the water—as if heaven and earth weren't moved to bring it to her.

"Can we ride on her?" asks the bigger boy.

More children gather around Trixie, watching her drink and snort and swish her tail.

"I want a ride, too," says the little girl.

That is followed by another chorus of voices asking the same thing. Amidst shouts of "Me! Me!" I clap my hands. I look around at the pied piper parade of kids.

I glance at Keston, who is tugging on his kite.

"Do you think it's okay for them to ride on Trixie? One by one."

"Sure, why not?"

My lawyer brain can think of a hundred reasons why not.

"Where's your mother?" I ask the two boys who brought the bowl. "I'd like to thank her."

And make sure it's okay for them to take a ride on Trixie's back.

"Momma's over there," he points to a lady in a turban cutting up a large bed sheet.

Four preteens hold a corner each, pulling the sheet taut.

"What is she doing?" I stand up to watch her zip a sharp pair of scissors along the cloth.

All the kids surrounding me shout, "Making kite tails."

I nod as if I understand. "By cutting up your bedding? That seems rather drastic."

"Old sheets," a little girl says. "She's getting the tails ready for the kites you have in there." A stubby brown finger pokes my garbage bag of Keston's kites.

"Oh, right," I smile at the child. "That makes sense."

"Hey Kes, when are you handing out the kites?"

But he doesn't hear me. His beautiful Megatron is zipping, dipping, and falling out of the sky.

"Watch out!" He waves his arms to clear the field. Megatron could hurt someone.

"Come on, kids," I shout, running for cover under the trees lining the field. I count the children as they swoop in. Twelve, no thirteen, small faces stare up at me, waiting for further instructions.

I gather my wits and say as if I've been leading kids all my life.

"Once the danger is clear, we will take turns patting and riding on Trixie."

"Okay," they say in unison.

I'm still holding the little girl's hand. She smiles a gap-toothed smile up at me.

You got this, CJ.

Trixie trots up to join us, hee-hawing the whole way. Either she's happy I can do this. Or she's pissed she hasn't gotten her snacks as yet. Let's hope it's the first one.

Chapter Eighteen

The giant kite almost falling out of the sky is the highlight of St. Nicholas Day.

Megatron does not fall. But only because several men abandon their own kites and race to help Keston keep it from plunging to earth.

They run like madmen helping Kes reel in the kite thread. They don't seem concerned they're giving up their chances at winning.

Everyone is screaming and jumping up and down, including me and the thirteen children, as Megatron spirals a few times on the brink of falling.

The crowd claps and cheers when Megatron finally climbs high into the blue sky, fluttering its black and blue wings like an ascending angel.

I wipe the blurry tears from my eyes. It feels like an Olympic moment. One athlete is getting help from his competitors.

"Are you okay, miss?" A little boy asks.

I nod. "Yes, I'm great."

This is what Keston was talking about. The spirit of the island. To help each other.

I'm going to spend the rest of the day trying to embody the same energy, starting with the kids.

"Who's ready to go for a donkey ride?" I shout.

Little arms shoot up and wave in the air.

"Okay, form lines, we're taking turns."

I take Trixie's reins and lead her out from under the tree.

"Hey, girl, we're going to make many children happy today, okay."

She gives me her wide, picket-toothed smile.

"Hee-haw!" she brays.

"You need help, miss?" asks a deep sing-song voice behind me.

I swing around to find Keston's handsome brother, Kelley. He has an otherworldly beauty.

Kelley lives on the other side of the island on a farm where he grows everything he eats, drinks, and wears. He's a self-contained unit. He doesn't have any concept of money.

Whenever I offer to buy some of his beautiful handmade clothes, he shushes me and gives them to me as presents.

Keston suggested I give Kelley a gift as payment. It was hard to figure out what to give someone who has everything and doesn't use commercial goods.

He weaves his socks, makes his toothbrush and toothpaste, and doesn't own a mirror.

In the end, I brought a gorgeous coffee table book from New York with photographs of locations and landmarks from around the world.

Kelley loved it. He kissed the book after carefully wrapping up the paper it came in.

Now, I throw my arms around his neck and hug him.

It is my personal opinion that Kelley does not get enough human contact living as he does all alone with cows and goats and a bunch of hemp plants.

You never know when he'll show up. He's the hermit of St. Nicholas.

"I would love your help," I say truthfully. I wondered how I'd keep all the kids busy while I walked Trixie up and down.

Kelley takes Trixie's makeshift reins and hoists the little girl up on her back.

Her eyes are round saucers as she concentrates on staying upright.

"What's your name?" I ask.

"Alicia Elizabeth Charles," she says. "But you can call me Alice."

I grin at her. "What a lovely name, Alice."

Some kids standing in line call out, "Giddy up, Alice. Go fast."

But Alice is having none of that cowboy stuff.

"Shhh," she says, patting Trixie's back. "Don't listen to them."

Kelley walks off with the first child.

Keston is far down the field, still holding onto Megatron.

This time, he has the help of two strong teenagers. The way they're struggling with the wind blowing Megatron this way and that, I'm not sure if they're flying the kite or the kite is flying them.

"Is it my turn next?" asks the little boy who gave Trixie water.

I assure him he will ride next. "What is your name?"

"Jason."

"Okay, Jason. Get ready, here they come."

Kelley returns with Trixie and Alice. I take Alice off the donkey, and Kelley hoists Jason up next.

The line of children is growing behind me. Pretty soon, they may get tired of waiting around, and then what?

My heartbeat speeds up. How will I handle a group of unruly kids? Keston will see I can't do it, and everyone will see I'm a phony.

I stare at all their upturned faces. They look at me expectantly. As if they believe I have the answers.

I wish I could call Giselle for advice.

My voice is shaky as I say, "Why don't we all sit together as we wait our turn."

Fifteen children collapse as one.

I join them on the grass.

Maybe the secret to not feeling like an imposter is to show up and try.

I say the first thing that comes to my head.

"Who's ready for their kites?"

The smiles breaking across their little faces fill me with joy.

"Okay, let me grab the kite bag."

And that's how I spend the rest of St. Nicholas Day. I hand out kites, help Jason's mother cut up bedsheets to make kite tails, and give donkey rides to every child there.

By the time the races are underway, the kite flying is over, and Trixie rests on the grass; I am exhausted, grass-stained, and hungry.

But I have not complained once.

"Way to go, my future wife," Keston says, finding me in the crowd watching the sack races.

I lean against my tall, handsome man. "You wouldn't believe the day I've had."

"I would, sweetheart. I saw it all. You're a star."

I smile like a child with a new kite.

Chapter Nineteen

My and Keston's lovemaking has always been wild, unpredictable, and steamy.

It can happen any and everywhere, at the drop of a hat. Or rather at the drop of my panties.

His desire to please me in and out of the bedroom has been the driving force of our relationship.

Well, that and his charming nature and conviction that we belong together.

But tonight, after we are all safely home — Trixie and I got a ride in the back of a friend's pickup truck — I see a side of Keston I've never seen before.

We're lying in bed, all clean and fresh and sweet smelling. I'm not sure what to expect. He's lying across the bed with his feet propped up on the wall, so I lay like that, too.

He starts recapping the day.

I can't believe he's talking to me about kites instead of ravaging my body.

My mind is spinning with questions.

Is something wrong here? Has he gotten tired of our everyday sex life? Is this the part where we become like an old married couple?

I don't know about him, but I'm not ready for it to stop. I love the playful, spontaneous man I fell in love with.

"Is everything okay?" I ask.

He turns his head and smiles. "Of course, babe."

I'm dying to ask why aren't you kissing me? Or better yet, why aren't you kissing my pussy. But I stop myself.

You do not want to sound desperate, CJ. Get a grip. You had sex this morning.

Usually, he counts the hours between sessions.

"Earth to CJ." Keston waves a hand in front of my face.

"I'm here. Just thinking."

He smiles lazily. "Come over here; you're too far away."

He slides an arm under my shoulders and cuddles me to him. I run my fingers up and down his washboard abs.

"I was so proud of you today, babe," he says. "You showed the entire community you can do anything. And you looked like you were having fun."

"I was."

"I never thanked you for moving to St. Nicholas. For making this your home. I've been thinking about all you sacrificed to be here with me. And I want you to know how happy I am to share my life with you."

He turns dark, soulful eyes on me. "You're one of a kind, CJ."

"Thank you?" I feel a blush staining my cheeks.

"Which is why . . . ." he stops and holds my gaze like *forever.*

My heart starts beating too fast for its cavity. It wants to escape and run around the room a few times.

"Why what?" My voice trembles. Something is wrong. He's a man of action. Where are all these words coming from?

He climbs over my body, kneels on the floor, and takes my hand.

From my viewpoint, he's upside down and too far from my honeypot.

What the fuck is happening? Is this a new sexual position? How is he going to reach my pussy from way over there?

"Carmela Anne Jones, my darling, my love, my star in the sky with diamonds. I have something very important to say. I almost don't know how to say it." His voice catches.

My legs drop from the wall like two logs rolling down a river.

"Are you crying? What's going on, Keston? Are you breaking up with me?"

I shift my entire body around so I can face him. I hear my heart thumping in my chest. Please God, don't let this man break up with me.

"Is it because of Marcus being Lucy's father?" I cry.

"What? No!"

"Then what is it? Why are there tears in your eyes? Keston Kips, talk to me right now."

I scoot up on my knees. "Is it because I'm a lot older than you?"

His tears have disappeared. "No!"

"Then what is it? You're making me crazy!"

"Can you be quiet for one minute? I'm trying to ask you to marry me."

"Don't tell me to be quiet. Wait. *What?*"

"Woman, give me your damn hand. Sheesh. A man can't even get romantical with you."

"Romantical?" I giggle. "That's not a word."

"It is in this house. Now, Carmela Anne Jones, also known as CJ, please be quiet and listen."

I nod silently. Tears prick my eyelids. Is this happening?

I remember the last time I thought I was being proposed to. It was back in March, nine months ago.

It was my birthday dinner with Marcus. I tried to sneak out my phone to videotape the special moment.

But that's the last thing I want to do now.

"I'm listening," I say solemnly, my slim fingers resting in his big, strong hand.

He turns over my hand and strokes my palm. He raises shiny eyes to my face.

"You and your happiness are the most important things in my life."

My heart flutters wildly.

He reaches under the mattress and pulls out a small red box. It's hand-carved like he made it himself. My heart soars as he opens the box to reveal a ring of the most intricate design.

It's a silver sculpted ring of tiny flowers, with a bright blue-green stone the color of the Caribbean Sea in the center of each flower.

"It's stunning," I breathe reverently.

He breaks into a smile. "Kelley and I made it. Well, he did, but I told him what I wanted."

"You made this ring?"

He nods. "For you. The stone is larimar, a rare gem found only in the Caribbean. It enhances true love. If soulmates meditate with the larimar stone, they build deeper connections. This is why I chose this stone for your ring. You are my soul mate, CJ, and I want to spend the rest of our lives together, building a deeper connection."

Before he finishes speaking, tears roll down my face. All my adult life, I wondered if I'd ever meet the man for me. Now, here he is, and he feels the same way. And he made this fabulous ring. Well, he *designed* it.

"Can I put it on?" I'm bouncing on my knees, excitement coursing through my entire body.

He retakes my hand. "CJ, will you be my wife? Will you . . . ."

"Oh my God, yes!"

I throw myself into his arms. Luckily, he catches me.

He covers my face with kisses. Then, he slides the ring on my finger. I stretch out my hand to admire it.

"It's perfect. Absolutely perfect."

"There's no turning back now, woman. You're mine."

I giggle. "Can you believe we made it this far?"

His dark curls shake from side to side. "I knew it the moment I met you. It just took you forever to catch up."

My lips press tightly together so I don't bawl.

"What do we do now?" I ask. "Should we call people?"

I don't know about him, but I'm dying to video chat with my girls.

As if reading my mind, Kes says, "You can tell everyone tomorrow. Tonight, you are mine."

He lays me down on the bed and unbuttons my nightshirt.

"Now, let's see what I can do to my fiancee, which I haven't already tried."

"Nothing," I laugh. 'You've done it all."

He gives me a dashing look. "Are you kidding? We're just getting started. Now come here, and let me spoil my bride-to-be."

Chapter Twenty

I don't know if it's because I am deliriously happy or because I'm in a state of shock, but when Keston enters me with his powerful cock, fireworks explode in the night sky.

"Wow! Look at what you made happen."

I wrap my legs around his waist and raise my hips to take every inch of him.

He moves slowly, deeply, in the most intimate lovemaking of my life.

"Thanks," he says. "But that's the St. Nicholas Day's fireworks finale."

"Nice. Can you make that happen down there?" I click my tongue to indicate what I mean.

He grabs my wrists and stretches them above my head, holding them there firmly. I don't have much wiggle room.

He lays one heavily muscled thigh on top of one of my legs. Now I really can't move.

"I'm claustrophobic," I cry, feeling trapped and loving it.

He rotates his hips as if he's doing that soca wine dirty dancing they do down here. Nice and slow. Deeper and deeper.

"Are you stirring a drink?"

He covers my mouth with his own. "Hush."

His penis grazes my G spot. I gasp.

"Oh, you like that?" His eyes gleam. His cock sinks deeper still. I can feel it in my womb.

Despite his weight on top of me, I raise my hips to meet his thrusts.

"Good thing I do yoga," I say.

"Good thing."

I pump my hips in rhythm to his deep, circular motion. The headboard hits the wall. Over and over.

"This is like the Beenie Man song," I say, sweat gliding down my neck.

"Which one?" His breath comes faster as his hips move at high speed like a powerful engine.

His hand flutters downward between my legs, and he rubs my clit in time to his thrusts.

"Oh, God," I moan. "Just like that, baby."

"Which song?" he asks again.

My brain empties of everything but how good this feels.

"Doesn't matter," I wheeze.

"The one where she wants a guy with the wickedest slam?" he asks, eyes gleaming brighter as he slams his thick cock into my weeping pussy.

I can't answer. I'm in ecstasy. I want this and more.

I feel excitement building in my stomach, ready to overflow.

He eyes me with a devilish grin. "That song?"

I nod wildly. "Yes, yes."

He drives his cock into my pussy like a jackhammer. Over and over. His fingers rub my clit in perfect synchronization.

I am riding a wave as high as a kite.

His shaft gets larger inside me. It expands and gets heavy like a balloon you fill with water.

"I'm going to burst," he says.

"Do it," I pant.

But he doesn't want to come until I do. He slows down his pumping and pulls out until just the tip is rubbing against my pussy walls.

It's so lonely inside me now.

"Put it back," I cry.

He bites his lips and eases it all the way in.

The nerve endings around my clit dance for joy.

His hips swivel and dip, then swivel and dip some more; it's the oldest rhythm known to man—the rhythm of sex.

My body floats higher and higher, reaching for something untouchable.

With one hand holding down my arms and one hand stroking my pussy, Keston rams his big cock deep to my core. Just the way Beenie Man sings about.

A low whimper escapes my mouth.

The edge of nowhere is approaching. I'm almost to the top.

The wave starts slowly, then builds into a tsunami.

WHAM!

This orgasm is like nothing I've felt in my life. Fireworks explode in the sky outside and inside my chest.

The scream I hear is primal and full of every emotion— the good, the bad, and the ugly.

It reaches my soul and squeezes me to my tiniest atom.

"I'm coming too," he cries out.

He lets go of my hands. I clutch his body to mine as the headboard smacks the wall. The mattress groans. Kes's dick is a fast-moving piston. His strong thrusts rock me back and forth, sending me straight to heaven once again.

"Holy smokes!"

Kes grunts. His hot cum fills me like a river of light.

"Good God, woman. Whenever I think I've got you figured out, you raise the stakes."

A slow smile spreads over my face. I tweak his nipples.

"Ouch!"

There's more where that came from, I want to say.

But in the spirit of our recent engagement, I let him have the last word.

Just this once.

Afterwards, we snuggle together on the bed. He kisses the tip of my nose and drifts off to sleep.

I can't sleep. My mind is whizzing and full of thoughts about our engagement.

Right now, I wish I had recorded the event. So I could look at it over and over.

I almost don't believe I'm engaged.

I stare at the ring and hold up my hand, turning it this way and that. He and Kelley created a masterpiece. It's a one-of-a-kind stunning ring that reflects our unique relationship.

I remember the first night on No Man's Land when I was scared and couldn't sleep.

We barely knew each other, but Keston handed me a night-blooming flower with the most delicious scent to help me fall asleep.

I stare at his handsome face under the light of the moon shining through the curtains.

"My husband," I whisper.

I said I'd tell everyone tomorrow, but I can't wait. I snap a photo of the ring and send it to a group chat with my girls.

"I'm engaged!"

Then I send a text and photo to my mother.

My phone immediately lights up with messages of congratulations and love.

"You're going to marry the man of your dreams," Mikah writes.

"Finally, CJ, you are going to have it all. A wonderful husband. A beautiful home on a gorgeous island. Hopefully, children will be in your future. I'm so happy for you." That is from Giselle.

Mom sends her love but writes, "The only thing missing is a new career."

I send her a thumbs-up. She's right.

I have to find a purpose for my life. I can't read romance novels and play with Trixie all day.

I need to find and follow my passion. Like how Kelley is creating a unique lifestyle.

And how Keston is not only a supreme mixologist but created a book of rum drinks that is gaining popularity all over the world.

If I'm fortunate, I can make money doing what I love too.

Good thing I had my flash of inspiration right before I fell on Gang Gang Sarah's grave.

Maybe the inspiration came from her. Maybe she's not to be feared but to be honored.

One thing I've learned from being stranded on No Man's Land. A bad situation can reap great benefits. It's all about what you make of it.

Chapter Twenty-One

The next morning, I awake with a feeling of excitement.

Kes is not in the bed, but the ring is still on my finger, so it wasn't a dream.

Where the hell is my fiancé?

I can't wait to find him to tell him the idea I've been mulling over all week while I waited for St. Nicholas Day to come and go.

This idea could be a great business, and it may be my passion as a new St. Nicholas Islander.

I fall out of the sheets and land on the floor with a thud.

"Kes!" I cry out.

A loud banging noise from the porch tells me he's either building something or Trixie is up to no good.

I hurry and wash up, get dressed in my cutest romper (I am a newly engaged woman, after all!), and grab a cup of espresso from the kitchen.

The loud banging continues.

"Trixie," I shout. "That better not be you making a mess out there."

I turn to exit the kitchen and come face to face with my donkey.

"*Arrrgh!*" I scream. "Why are you in here? This is unhygienic."

Trixie snorts.

"Sorry," I reply. "I don't mean to imply that you're dirty."

She smiles and nudges my shoulder.

"But you *are* a farm animal," I mutter under my breath so she doesn't hear me.

Trixie seems to care less what I say or think. She blinks at me with her incredibly long eyelashes.

"Fine. I'll give you carrots."

But there's none in the fridge or the veggie bin.

I search around in the bare cupboards.

Kes and I need to do some grocery shopping.

So far, we've been eating fresh vegetables we get from Kelley's farm and fish from the fishermen.

I've brought enough Nespresso capsules to last months.

Kes buys fresh milk and eggs from a nearby farmer. I pick up tea bags at the gourmet grocery store in the resort.

And, of course, he gets his bottles of rum from winning island competitions like he did again yesterday with Megatron.

But a bag of potato chips or Oreos wouldn't be bad. A little variety won't kill us.

Trixie waits patiently, blocking the doorway.

I rummage around in the fridge again. "How about an old apple?"

I cut out the bruised dark spots and feed her apple slices. She shoves her nose into my hand and munches on everything: the core, seeds, and stem.

"Can I go now?"

Another loud snort, and we're headed to the porch. Trixie is a happy pet. I require caffeine.

As I guessed, Keston is outside. He's shirtless, sweaty, and slamming coconuts with his machete onto a cement block to crack them open.

Kind of like chopping wood. But louder.

"What are you doing?" Although it is clear what's taking place.

"I mean, why are you cutting open all these coconuts." I eyeball the pile on one side of him and husks on the other.

He wipes his brow with his bandana. Can he be any sexier?

"Harvesting the coconuts," Kes explains. "I climbed the trees and cut them down so they don't fall on your precious head. Or on Trixie's. Or anyone walking by."

"Who walks by here? We live in the boonies."

He frowns. "The what?"

I wave a hand. "You know, far away from civilization."

"She means behind God's back," Kelley says, shimmying down from a tree.

Kelley strides up beside Keston, linen pants hanging low on his hips. His tanned, bare torso screams. "I'm the hottest man alive."

"Hey guys, get closer together, I want to take a picture."

The two men, blood enemies just a month ago, are now friends. Thanks to my search for the Kipson pirate treasure.

I snap pictures of the brothers in the yard chopping open coconuts, pouring the coconut water into large jugs, and then piling the husks and covering them with a tarp for later use as firewood.

Wait until Mikah sees what she's missing!

They are two hella swoon-worthy men.

Kelley has a much lighter complexion than Keston, and his curls are reddish-blond instead of black, but they could be twins.

"Kelley!" I wave to my future brother-in-law. "I didn't

get to thank you yesterday for helping with the kids and Trixie."

He nods. "I enjoyed it. Let me know if you ever need me to do that again."

"Okay," I say. Although, when will that ever happen? Next year?

I walk down the steps into the bright sunshine. I blink hard to be able to see again.

"Also, I want to thank you for this." I wave my hand about in the air. The sun catches the larimar gems, and the jewelry sparkles like the bright blue sea on my hand.

"Wow!" I hold my hand and stare at my finger. "Did you guys see that?"

The brothers stare at me in a similar, confused manner.

"The ring, duh! The way it glitters and shines in the sun."

"Oh," Kelley smiles. "Congratulations. You like the ring."

"I love the ring."

I slip an arm through Keston's sweaty, dirty arm. And I complained about Trixie! "We're going to be married," I sing song.

"When?" asks Kelley in his no-nonsense way.

"Yeah, when?" Kes echoes, winking at me.

I smile in what I hope is a mysterious manner. "When the time is right."

Kelley blinks. "Humans put pressure on time to be more than it is."

Keston, on the other hand, jokes. "Don't make me wait

too long, woman." His mouth slides up on one side into a crooked smile.

That right there is the difference between the brothers.

They have the same square-jawed, chiseled face, juicy lips, and body type.

But they are miles apart in personalities. While Kes is a playful, happy man, Kelley is serious and literal. He rarely jokes around.

But his sincerity is what I love about him. He is solid, strong, and incredibly persistent.

He's the perfect man for Mikah. If I can get my business idea going, they will be the first couple I bring together.

"Kes, what are you doing after the harvest?"

He blinks. "What do you need? I have the whole day off."

Chapter Twenty-Two

Several hours later, Keston and I are flying over the turquoise sea in his powerboat, which I still have to name.

The last time we were in this boat was a traumatic experience involving a late-night pirate treasure hunt.

It feels like just yesterday I was battling a sea monster and saving his life.

I give him a giddy smile now.

He pinches my butt.

We exchange a quick kiss as he steers the boat around the waves. Our relationship has not run the usual course of dating disasters. Like spilling a drink on him, or him forgetting to call when he said he would.

Or one of us (me!) falling asleep while the other is talking. All mini-dramas that test a new bond.

Our relationship has been more like a Netflix series of life-threatening events.

This afternoon, I'm keeping my fingers crossed for a near-perfect day.

When Keston slows down to glide over the reefs, the sun's rays beam down, revealing an underwater world of dramatic vistas.

I perch on the edge of the seat, arms spread wide to keep from falling in. Although I wouldn't mind swimming with the rainbow fish nibbling on the pink and purple rocks.

The tropics favor bold, bright colors, especially pinks and purples.

From sunrises and sunsets to coral reefs and flowers.

No wonder these are my new favorite shades for decorating the cottage.

Living in this multi-hued world of waterfalls and grottos can change your perspective that black and grey tones are classic.

Like now, Keston's not-trying-at-all combination of a tie-dye tank and beachy shorts would not fly in New York. Not even at Rockaway Beach.

But here, they are perfect for a day on the sea, even if his clashing colors scream for an intervention by the fashion police.

Keston is oblivious or could care less, and that's what counts.

As for me, I maintain my fashion sense with cute swimsuits, cover-ups and matching sandals.

Today, however, I'm wearing cut-off shorts and a tee shirt because we have some trekking to do. And I want to be ready for anything.

I'm so busy contemplating the differences between my old and new lives that I take my eyes off the water.

Something I've learned to be dangerous when boating in the open sea.

Waves can be unpredictable. They rise like dragons from the deep, ready to swallow you at any moment.

Even the best captains can't avoid every unexpected roller on the sea.

Our boat skims off the top of a wave and dips low into a trough just as another wave comes out of nowhere.

It smacks me in the face with warm salt water. My shirt is soaked.

"Ooomph!" I grunt as some more splashes in my mouth.

I scoot back from the edge.

"What the hell?" I exclaim.

'Sorry," Keston shouts over the noise of the engine.

He looks so happy to be in his boat, I don't want to

complain. Plus, my brand new business idea involves being in this boat and traveling this same route, so I'd better get used to it.

"Wham!" Another wave soaks us.

Seriously!

"Sorry, babe."

He doesn't look sorry. He looks even happier.

I dry my face with a beach towel.

"You're doing it on purpose," I grumble.

He stares at my chest, where my nipples are outlined under the damp shirt.

"Why would I want to get your tee shirt wet on purpose?" He grins like a bad boy.

I give him a side-eye. "Don't make me hurt you."

He throws a kiss my way. "I love you, babe."

Keston's philosophy in life is to kiss all things right.

Mine is to analyze everything.

"Yeah, sure," I say grouchily. I tap my fingers on the dashboard. Maybe I need to learn how to drive the boat myself.

Since my new business will involve boat rides, I can't expect Keston always to be available.

Hmmm. I hadn't thought of that.

The only other person I know who can drive this powerboat and is not a working fisherman is Tabitha, Keston's ex-girlfriend.

I can't ask her. Although we have a bit of a truce, I don't trust her.

She might still be waiting me out. Hoping I'll leave the island so she can swoop back into Keston's arms.

I wouldn't put it past her to leave me stranded on No Man's Land. "Over my dead body," I mutter.

"What, babe?' he asks.

"Nothing."

Out of the corner of my eye, I glimpse winged creatures whizzing by the boat—lots of them.

I can't believe what I'm seeing.

"Flying fish," Kes says.

About twenty winged fish soar alongside the boat.

"They're really flying," I exclaim. Now I've seen it all. Their wings are flat and sparkly gossamer.

One flies over the bow of the boat. Others fly alongside us for a distance before dropping back into the sea.

"That's amazing," I say, thoughts of Tabitha's potentially wicked plans replaced by nature's never-ending wonders.

"They're delicious, too. We can catch some on the way home. For dinner tonight."

"We can't eat them. They're cute."

"Everything is cute to you."

"Not true. You're barely tolerable."

Kes grabs me up and hauls me in front of his body to stand between his legs. His arms encircle me to reach the steering console. The heat from his body burns me.

"You're going to say you're sorry." He pokes me with his manhood.

"Or else?" I lean back against him feeling his cock grow harder as it presses on my ass.

I can't help the smile that grows on my face.

"Knowing I can turn you on so fast is nice," he says.

"Honey, it's more like figuring out how to turn me off. I am always on around you."

"Ha!" he laughs. "You're forgiven."

He nuzzles my neck, grips the steering wheel with one hand, and wraps his other arm around my chest, holding me close.

"Lean back and enjoy the ride," he whispers.

Chapter Twenty-Three

We pass miles of emerald green hills surrounding curved white sandy bays that are inaccessible except by boat.

We're heading toward a place I never thought I'd want to see again.

No Man's Land.

The uninhabited island, part of the St. Nicholas Islands chain of tiny islets and cays, is where I had the scariest moments of my life—but also the best ones.

It's where Keston and I survived for days and fell in love. It's also where we almost died when a hurricane roared in.

I would love to help other potential couples fall madly in love on a deserted island—minus the deathly hurricane conditions, of course.

As Keston steers the boat up to the sandy end of the beach, my heart shuffles through a mixed deck of feelings.

I'm curious about how the island looks after the hurricane's damage abated.

There were many fallen trees, and the gorgeous waterfall where I had the best times had turned into a mud pit.

I'm also sad that my favorite coconut tree had been pulled out of its sandy roots and toppled over.

I'll have to find another beloved tree to host beach picnics. Starting with the picnic I have in store today in Keston's old, beat-up cooler.

I understand his desire not to replace anything unless it's completely useless, but this cooler looks like it came from an American G.I. in World War II. The words "Property of the U.S. Army" are carved on its side.

He says it washed up on his beach. But it's time for a pink Yeti cooler.

Since we had no groceries at home, Kes boated up to the dock of the closest village before we set out.

We grabbed snacks and two bottles of wine and stuffed

the cooler with a bag of ice that is now leaking very cold water on my feet.

Yup. I'll have to buy a new cooler if I want to run an exclusive boat and picnic tour for discerning couples.

Keston turns the boat around and backs onto the sandy beach. He leaps out, throws his anchor in the front, and drags a line to tie up to a coconut tree. I watch it all and wish I had a notebook to write notes for when I may have to do it alone.

I shiver at the thought of all these hardcore physical tasks.

I did not train for this. My brain is the only thing that got any exercise at work.

"You ready, princess?' he asks, holding out a hand to help me ashore.

I weigh my desire to let him carry me off the boat against my need to be self-sufficient for future trips.

"I can do it. Turn around."

"Why?"

"In case I fall and blotch my graceful exit."

He frowns. "Just let me help you. I'm not going to stand here and watch you hurt yourself."

"It's what mothers must do when their babies are learning to walk."

His frown deepens. "Am I the mother in this scene?"

"Yes. And I am a newbie. Now turn around."

He sits down on a coconut tree stump. It looks like Prince Harry, my beloved tree that died to save us.

"I am not turning around," he says calmly, bending a knee across one leg.

"And if you look like you'll fall, I *am* going to catch you. Sorry if that makes me a terrible mother."

His tone gets a bit edgy. I can see he'll make a stubborn parent.

"Fine. But only because that is what I'd do too."

"Great. Hurry up, I'm hungry. You didn't come all the way here to practice leaping out of our boat, did you?"

"Actually, yes, I did."

He shakes his black curls. They glisten with drops of water. "You're so weird."

"And you're so annoying."

I leap out in one swift jump. I land on the sand with one ankle almost giving way.

Keston grabs my arms and hauls me straight up so no weight falls on the ankle.

"Good save," I grumble. "I have a weak ankle."

"You're welcome."

He reaches into the boat and easily retrieves the cooler.

"Damn!"

"What?" he looks around, alarmed. "Are you okay?"

"I should have put the cooler on the bow before jumping out. I wish I had a notebook to write down this entire procedure."

He swings the cooler from one hand and takes my hand in his other.

"Please tell me what's going on. I feel you've left me out of an entire conversation you had with yourself on our way here."

He knows me so well.

"I do have a plan. I'll tell you when we're sitting down."

"Are you going to draw an outline of your plan in the sand again?" He smirks.

I suck my teeth. "Maybe."

As we stroll down the beach, I catch glimpses of our time here. A piece of Keston's bright red bandana tied to a stick.

The makeshift grill is still propped up against a tree, but wild grass is growing all over it.

A lump forms in my throat. Goosebumps of nostalgia raise on my arms.

"Keston, look."

I point to a circle in the sand where a bonfire once was lit. By me.

Remnants of twisted yarn and the spine of a book are still visible, tumbled together with coconut tree leaves I burned.

"I thought the sea would have washed it all away. But it's still here."

"No one comes here anymore. The Cocoa Reef Resort stopped their catamaran boat trips. They go to another closer island instead."

He stares at the bonfire with no sign of remembering it. But he wouldn't. He was unconscious.

I did this to save us. Which is why I know I can make my idea work. I can do whatever I put my mind to. This is proof.

Kes pokes a stick at the burnt material. "Is that the romance book you were reading aloud for me?"

I swallow around the lump in my throat.

"It is."

Suddenly, a reel of our last day on this island plays full color in my head.

"Oh, Kes. I don't know if I can do it."

"What?" He drops the cooler and rushes to my side. "What is it, baby? Tell me."

But I can't speak. I cover my face with my hands to stop the images rocking me to my core.

"We almost died here," I whisper.

"But we didn't. Thanks to you." He rubs circles on my back and croons softly in my ear. "I'll never forget how amazing you were then and still are. You can do anything."

His hand rubbing my back soothes me. I gulp down any tears threatening to fall.

"You really think that? You don't think I'm a spoiled New Yorker who complains and whines?"

He sits back on his heels. "Of course, you're a spoiled New Yorker who complains and whines. But that's not *all* you are."

I push him. He plops backwards onto the sand. "Thanks."

"You're welcome." He unlatches the cooler and takes out one bottle of wine. "Shoot, we forget the glasses."

I grimace. "It's going to be like the last time we were here. We will have to drink from a coconut shell, huh?"

He uncorks the wine in two seconds. "No, because we will drink from the bottle like . . . ." He squints at me.

"Lovers?" I suggest.

"Like a happily married couple."

I laugh. You're jumping ahead. We've only been engaged one day."

He hands me the bottle to take the first sip. "We can practice."

I smile at that. "Okay, here's to being happily married. In the future."

"Hey, CJ, what is that idea you said you'd tell me about."

I dig in the cooler for the cheese and crackers.

I set up the cheese board on my knees and borrow Keston's ever-ready pocket knife to cut chunks of cheese.

Then, I feed him a cracker with cheese and a bit of guava jam.

"This is it. This is my idea."

"What?"

"Couples having picnics on this beach."

He nods. "I love it. We're doing it."

Chapter Twenty-Four

S tarting a business is hard, like starting anything: a new job, a new exercise regimen, and definitely a new romance.

But setting up *True Love Trips*, the name Kes and I settled on as we sat on the beach at No Man's Land, drinking white wine and discussing my idea, is not just hard work. It's a lot of fun.

"I've never been happier," I tell Trixie, who is snoozing by my feet on the porch while I finish creating the website and social media pages from online tutorials.

It's the last bit. Other than getting customers to sign up for the trips.

I can't believe we got everything done in one week.

When I explained my idea of creating meaningful experiences for couples on No Man's Land, with an exciting boat ride to the island and then privacy to connect or reconnect over a gourmet picnic, Kes got so excited, he ran with it.

"You can do it, CJ. I'll help with whatever you need. So will Kelley."

Kes suggested the name *True Love Trips*. "Let's call it what it is—nice and simple. But if you want it set up before Christmas, you need to start tomorrow. The government offices close for the holidays. Christmas is a big thing here."

"Everything is a big event here. You guys don't need an excuse for a party."

"True," he happily agreed.

We were on our second bottle of wine by then and outlining the details we needed to make it a reality.

Kes was drawing diagrams in the sand with a stick.

"I'm going to call Tabitha to help you set everything up quickly," he said. She works for the government. She has all the connections."

"Uh . . . I'm not sure I want her involved with our business."

In fact, I *know* I don't want her involved.

He waved away my doubts about her. "She'll just help you set up the paperwork. Tabitha doesn't have to be involved in the day-to-day affairs."

I shivered at the words "Tabitha" and "affairs" in the same sentence. *Paranoid much, CJ?*

So, while I worked on creating an online presence, Kes took control of the business paperwork.

Three days later I held the official tourism business license and the incorporation papers. *True Love Trips* was real.

What made it even more real was that this morning, I found Kelley and Keston in the yard, painting the name *True Love Trips* on the side of the boat.

Kes beamed in the heat, paintbrush in hand. "What do you think?"

Kelley, who is an artist amongst his other professions—farmer, weaver, clothing designer, and carpenter—was painting tiny hearts, flowers, and coconut trees all around the name.

It looked simple, but it conveyed my idea of love, romance, beach, and fun.

"Oh my gosh, guys, it's beautiful." I snapped photos of it to share on social media.

Nothing was stopping us from creating a magical business based on love.

"Are you only catering to the rich and famous?" Kelley asked me in private.

"No, why?"

He'd turned bright red. I never knew Kelley could blush.

He's so down-to-earth and solid. Almost boring in his lack of drama.

When he did choose to do anything dramatic, it was intense—involving pirates and centuries-old mysteries.

Mikah admitted she adores Kelley's stability. It's what she needs in her life after her spying shenanigans.

"What is it, Kelley?" I asked.

He looked over his shoulder, probably to make sure Keston wasn't around.

"I'd like to do it. If you want to try it out on anyone."

"You and who?" I snapped a little too quickly.

It's not as if he and Mikah are in a relationship. She may be in love with him. But I don't know how he feels about her.

The one time I asked if he liked her, he clammed up.

Now, he stares at me. "The person I like." He said it as if it were obvious.

I was dying to ask who that was.

But can I start a business being a nosey parker? I can't interrogate my customers about their life or love choices.

This is an inclusive business. Everyone is welcome regardless of who their romance is with.

"Okay, Kelley. I would be happy to have you be the first customer."

Meanwhile, I was biting my tongue like crazy so I didn't blurt out, "Who do you love," like a teenager in the cafeteria.

Kelley nodded. "Let me know what else I can help with."

At that moment, Keston walked up with a wooden sign he and Kelley must have made this morning too.

The words, *True Love Trips*, were painted on it in the same script with the same flowers and hearts and trees.

"Where do you want me to hang this?" he asked. "Until we build you an official office over there." He pointed at a space next to the house but closer to the dock.

"You're building me an office?"

"We are," Kes said, pointing at his brother.

"We're really doing this, aren't we?" I said excitedly.

It was one thing to have an idea. It was another to see it coming together so fast.

"Yesterday, I ordered business cards and brochures from the local printer. The only thing left is to complete the website, start posting on social media, and buy pretty picnic baskets and a new cooler," I told the men.

"I'll make the picnic baskets for you," Kelley said. "I'll start them tonight."

"Kelley Kips baskets?"

Damn, these would be some iconic pieces of art being used to transport food and wine.

I gazed at my two sweet guys.

"Thank you," I said. I couldn't think of any other words to express my gratitude for their encouragement and belief in me.

Now, sitting on the porch with Trixie and putting the finishing touches on the website, I can't think of anything that could spoil my joy at helping others on their true love journeys.

"Trixie, my girl, we are going to change lives."

My daydream is interrupted by the cute ringtone I've put on since moving to the Caribbean. "*I feelin' hot hot hot.*"

I grab it without looking.

Keston's at work at the Cocoa Reef Resort. He's probably calling to ask if I'm still coming for happy hour.

He's creating new Christmas cocktails, and he wants me to try them out.

"Hi babe, I'm running late, but I'll be there."

"This is not '*babe*,'" says a voice I know well.

"Marcus?" My eyes open wide. I can think of only one reason he'd be calling and speaking in a disgusted tone of voice.

Lucy must have reached out to him.

"We have to talk," he says. "I'm on my way to St. Nicholas." He hangs up before I say a word.

The phone drops out of my hand and lands on Trixie's head. She leaps up in dismay.

"I'm sorry, Trix. I just got clobbered, too."

Chapter Twenty-Five

They say good things come in threes. Like the Three Wise Men, the Three Musketeers, and me, Keston and Trixie!

But do bad things also come in threes? I hope not.

I hope Marcus coming to St. Nicholas is a one-off and

does not kickstart Gang Gang Sarah's curse or whatever the islanders call it when you piss off one of their deities.

Marcus could piss anyone off by being a BWA. *Billionaire with Attitude.*

Everything is going so well with my romantic, business, and personal lives. I can't let Marcus screw them up.

To be fair, I must listen to whatever Marcus has to say. I can imagine his shock finding out he fathered a baby girl twenty years ago. I was in shock when she found me and I knew she existed.

But do I owe him more than a listening ear?

My bigger concern is how I will tell Keston that my ex, who he does not like, is coming to the island.

"Does not like" is putting it mildly. "What am I going to do, Trixie?"

The cute donkey snorts and whishes her tail to commiserate with me.

"I agree, Trix. We won't tell Keston anything. Let's focus on the business. When Marcus shows up, we can meet somewhere else and discuss whatever he wants to talk about, and then he'll leave, and that will be that."

Trixie shakes her head and bats her eyelashes at me as if to say, "You sure it'll go that way?"

"I hope." I pat her nose. "And if things get nasty, you've got my back, right?"

She winks at me.

"Great." I glance at her hooves. "How are your high kicks?"

She whines and puts her lips on my hand. It's code for "feed me now."

"Spoiled baby."

I reach into the fridge and unearth a few old carrots. I hold them out to her. They hang limply and unappetizingly. Even for a donkey.

I promise we'll get fresh ones."

Trixie rolls her eyes at me.

"Sorry, dude."

She turns and trots into the yard. I watch in disbelief as she beelines straight to my dresses hanging on the line.

"Don't you dare," I shout after her.

She ignores me.

"You better be here when I finish dressing for Happy Hour."

It's Friday, December 13th, and twelve days before Christmas. I'm not sure which one of these facts freaks me out the most.

That today is unlucky, Friday the 13th. And Marcus is on his way here. Or that it's only twelve days before Christmas.

Yours truly has not strung up one twinkly light, sent one holiday card, or bought one single gift for anyone.

"Trixie," I call nicely. "We need to get going."

I emerge from the cottage in my go-to happy dress. It's long and swirly with flowers embroidered around the hem.

It's the dress I imagined when I had to mentally block out the bad stuff happening on No Man's Land.

I found the fabric on the island. A local seamstress designed and made it for me. Once I'm a wage earner again, I'll order all my clothes from her.

Trixie trots over obediently. She knows the routine.

I flip a blanket on her back and throw the makeshift reins around her neck.

Ever since I rode her to town on St. Nicholas Day, I now ride her everywhere.

I, a fast-moving New Yorker who can zoom in and out of pedestrians like a Fast & Furious driver, now enjoy slow travel.

Trixie's side-to-side trotting relaxes me as I plan out business ideas.

I am more in touch with nature as I can smell the flowers and smile at the lizards. I even get up close and personal with wild animals like the cute agoutis living in the rainforest.

The best thing is that Trixie gets much-needed exercise.

The other day, Keston accused Trixie of "putting on size." That's island speak for "getting fat."

"You have to stop sharing your meals with her. She's not a pet," he said.

To which I responded, "Okay. I'm sorry."

But inside, I was shouting. "Maybe not to *you*."

I know the islanders think I'm strange because I choose to ride a donkey or a bike instead of buying a car or truck, as any normal person living here would.

They'd be partly right. The real reason is I'm poor.

I made partner at my law firm three years ago, and that

meant buying in as an equity partner, which translated to giving them all of my savings—every penny.

As a partner, you get a share of the firm's revenue. But by quitting, I am forsaking all that investment. Eventually, I hope to get some back. For now, I count every penny.

This is why my mother is concerned about me being jobless. She did not have an easy life, and her greatest fear was that I would struggle financially.

But since moving to St. Nicholas, I've never been happier.

Starting *True Love Trips* is positive and fulfilling. But I also need to make some bucks!

I settle onto Trixie's back, spreading the hem of my dress around my legs.

Trixie kicks up sand, rocks, and seashells as she does her two-step shuffle like a dancer on a Broadway stage.

I pull on her reins to direct her to turn right at the intersection.

She snorts happily.

She loves going to the Cocoa Reef Resort.

The tourists adore her.

They feed her the pineapple chunks and orange slices decorating their cocktails. It's no wonder she's gaining weight.

They ask to take my photo astride Trixie, having some far-fetched notion that this is how islanders commute.

I just want to get there in time to give my fiancé a big kiss and drink one of his amazing cocktails.

In honor of the holidays and all the tourists arriving from

their cold countries for a fun-in-the-sun vacation, Kes started a twelve-day Christmas cocktail challenge.

Every night until December 25th, he will be mixing a brand-new cocktail.

At the end of the twelve days, he's putting all the new recipes in a booklet to give to the guests to take home.

"Hurry, Trixie," I urge my slow-trotting donkey. "I don't want Keston to run out of his first Christmas cocktail."

I wonder what's going to be in it?

He mentioned a dark red flower called "sorrel," used to make holiday drinks by soaking the petals for days.

Trixie turns into the resort's long, curving driveway. She clip-clops on the cobblestones past the reception area, around the curved pathways, and straight to the beach bar.

"Baby," Kes rushes from behind the bar. "You made it." He helps me slide down Trixie's side.

"You look gorgeous in that dress."

I twirl around. The skirt spreads out wide.

"We could have a picnic on that thing," he teases. "Did you leave any fabric for the other women?"

I roll my eyes.

He kisses my nose. "You're cute as hell. Imagine what I can do to you under that parachute."

Before he gets any ideas, I ask for my specialty cocktail.

The sooner he gets behind the bar, the better it will be for me. I'm biting my tongue so I don't spill the news about Marcus coming here.

Kes brings the drink in a frosty glass with what looks and smells like nutmeg sprinkled on top.

"Is this sorrel?" I ask.

He shakes his head. "The sorrel petals are still soaking. This is our version of your egg nog."

I take a small sip. The creamy rummy drink is delicious. The rush of cold and spice makes my eyeballs pop wide.

"Wow, Keston."

He grins. "It's called *Punch de Creme*. You must make it at least one day before serving it for the flavors to blend well."

I nod and take a big sip of this delicious alcoholic milkshake. I grab a seat at the beach bar and kick off my sandals. My concerns about Marcus O'Brien disappear.

By my second glass of Keston's famous Punch de Creme, I'm singing along loudly to Mariah Carey's *"All I Want for Christmas is You."*

It's a fantastic beginning to the holidays. It even looks like Christmas here.

Twinkly lights blink on and off around the thatched bar roof.

More sparkly lights encircle the trunks of the coconut trees.

A nativity scene with life-like figures is set up under flowering bushes. Real lambs are tied to a fence around the manger. They munch on grass and *baa* occasionally.

An orange and white cat meows and weaves in and around the lambs. The Wise Men hold mangoes, a pineapple, and guavas.

It's unusual but just right.

To top it off, I've got my gorgeous fiancé, my adorable donkey, my new favorite drink, and a business.

What can go wrong?

The beach bar celebration of the 12th night before Christmas gets louder as the night gets later.

Trixie is oblivious to the party horn tooting, the karaoke singing, and the African drumming on two wooden djembes drums.

Amidst the celebration, Trixie snuggles up next to the lambs, a perfect addition to the nativity scene.

I'm on my third (or fourth) delicious *Punch de Creme*. It's the best drink Keston Kips has ever created. There's a hint of spice and everything nice in it.

Like an unexpected Christmas present. It reminds me of Lucy. She'd love this.

After ten, the fishermen show up singing and swaying.

Keston's schoolmates and friends arrive, including his ex, Tabitha St. Clair.

The tourists and locals mingle with the waiters and other hotel employees who join in.

It's like one big office party, except it's on a beach, the balmy breeze ruffles my hair, and I'm barefoot in the sand.

"You look happy," Kelley says, sliding on a stool beside me.

"You came!" I kiss his cheek.

"Only because Keston called and threatened me," he says seriously.

We both glance at the man himself, who is showing Dex, his assistant bartender, how to churn up some more *Punch de Cremes*.

The crowd claps with approval when Dex holds up his blender of the yummy Christmas drink.

"Let me buy you one," I say.

Kelley shakes his head. "I'm driving."

"You don't drive. You don't even have a vehicle."

Kelley taps his fingers along the bar. "It's new."

"No way! What is it?"

Part of me is excited Kelley will be able to travel from the far end of the island to visit more often. The other part is jealous as hell.

"Does this have anything to do with the person you want to take on *True Love Trips*?" I ask.

"Leave my brother alone," says Keston, sliding a drink down the bar for Kelley. "I almost had to sell our firstborn to get him here tonight."

My jaw drops open. "Our . . . *what*?"

"I can't drink alcohol, Kes; I told you this is my first time driving."

"It's a mocktail," Keston says to Kelley.

"And you," he leans over and kisses my mouth closed, "don't look so surprised. I can't wait to have a little CJ running around, getting into trouble."

Kes slides away as quickly as he appears. Customers are clamoring for his attention up and down the bar.

"What's a mocktail?" Kelley asks, turning his drink around, sniffing and frowning like it's a bomb.

"It means no alcohol. Where do you live, under a rock?"

"Yes," Kelley says.

"Right, I recall Mikah telling me it's as remote as you can get without being on another island."

A faint smile crosses his lips. He's not a smiley person. In fact, he hardly shows any emotion.

He could be on the spectrum. No one has ever tested him.

All I know is that Mikah was excited about Kelley's farm, which was unprecedented for her. She's always calm, cool, and detached.

I used to think that, being a supermodel, she was too beautiful to be bothered by everyday life issues.

Now I know she's a spy trained to have ice in her veins.

"Mikah told me you made everything. Your home, the furniture, your clothing, food, *everything*. I'd love to see it. Now that we can drive there."

He sips the drink.

I wait for him to respond.

He doesn't. I stir my own drink and frown at the dregs on the bottom. Can I order a fourth (fifth?) one of these suckers, I wonder.

We sit in companionable silence. Well, *we're* silent. The bar rocks with people talking loudly, laughing, singing, and engaging in friendly debates.

I don't mind the noise, but Kelley's shoulders hunch around his ears. As if he's trying to block out the commotion with his body.

"Let's go sit over there," I suggest casually, pointing to the pool area. "This is much too noisy for me."

I signal to Keston that we're moving to the pool. He throws me a kiss. He's in his element, mixing up a new cocktail for the masses as they cheer him on.

My baby is such an extrovert, while his brother is the opposite. It's a testament to Kelley's affection for his brother that he's out here tonight.

He gathers his drink and coaster and follows me.

I stretch out on a chaise lounge close to the pool. We're in the shadows, but we can watch everything happening as if we're in the theater and everyone else is on the stage.

"Much better," I say."

"I like you, CJ."

"Really? I like you, too, Kelley."

I smile at him like a puppy that finally got attention. If I had a tail, I'd be wagging it.

I wait for him to say more, but he seems more interested in his *fake drink* than in me.

I guess that is that. I won't be getting any more information out of him tonight.

Chapter Twenty-Seven

I glance at the new phone in Kelley's hand. He bought it only to keep in touch with Mikah after she left last month. Before that, he was a literal hermit.

"Do you miss her?" I ask gently.

He shakes his head no.

My heart drops to my toes. Poor Mikah. She adores him. I wonder if I should tell her it's not going to happen for them.

Kelley puts his glass down next to his feet and rests his elbows on his knees.

"You can't miss something you have."

"What? I'm not following."

"Mikah," he looks at me like I'm missing a few marbles. Maybe I am after all those loaded Christmas cocktails.

"Pretend I'm five years old and explain it to me very slowly."

"Do you miss Keston right now?" he asks.

My eyes catch a glimpse of my handsome fiancé behind the bar. "Um . . . he's right there."

Kelley stands up and blocks my line of sight. "Do you miss him now?"

"Whoa, maybe I had too many drinks for real. Where is this going?"

"Just because you cannot see the one you love with your two eyes doesn't mean they are not with you."

He points at the starless sky. Clouds hover in chubby clusters. "You can't see the constellations tonight. They are still there."

"Oh, I get it."

"Our eyes see only a small amount of what's happening. But our hearts know the truth."

"That is deep."

No one has ever accused *me* of being deep. I'd rather understand his meaning before I misconstrue it.

"Are you saying you love Mikah?"

At that moment, two fishermen strum a melody on what looks like guitars but are smaller and have fewer strings. Their huge hands are amazingly delicate with the tiny strings.

A couple of people dance around, shaking maracas high and low, their rhythm perfectly in sync.

One man hits two sticks together while others tap spoons or lighters on glass bottles.

"What's going on?" I ask Kelley. "Some kind of spontaneous band?"

"It's parang."

"It's what?"

Kelley jumps up. "I've got instruments in my new truck. I'll be back."

I can't believe how energized he became at the sound of this *parang*.

I pull out my phone and spell the word phonetically in my search bar. The explanation comes quickly.

Parang is a traditional folk music that originated in Venezuela and is performed by St. Nicholas Islanders at Christmas. The instruments played in parang come from the indigenous people of South America. Some instruments have European and West African roots.

"The melee has begun," Keston says, ducking under the leafy palm tree to reach my side. He grabs my hand. "Come on, sweetheart."

"I'm waiting for Kelley," I tell him.

Truth is . . . I'm waiting for Kelley to answer my question about Mikah.

But Keston hauls me up and spins me around to the lively music.

It's hard to be stern with this man whose joy is like this never-ending song. Even if I don't understand the source of the music, I feel the beat in my bones.

Kes twirls me, pulls me close, kisses me, then spins me outward again.

"Don't let me fall into the pool," I pant.

"Never."

Kelley returns and presents me with a tambourine. It is beautifully made—another one of his creations.

He bestows on Keston something that looks like a flute.

Keston drops my hand to examine it. "Bro, is this our father's?"

Kelley blinks. "Not anymore. It's yours."

Keston hesitates. Then, he puts it to his lips and blows out the same sweet melody being played.

"I didn't know you played a musical instrument," I say.

"Woman, you watched me play my guitar."

"Oh yeah. Sorry, I forgot."

Truth is, with all that's been happening and at such a fast pace, there's a lot to process in my new life. I can't keep up with it all. I need a vacation to lie in a hammock and let it all sink in.

Plus, can I help it if these Kips' men do *everything*?

"Sheesh!" I grouch with a mixture of pride and disgust.

"Come on, let's join the melee," Keston says, guiding me with his hand on my lower back.

"What about you?" I shout over my shoulder to Kelley. "What do you play?"

He shakes his head. "I'm okay. And the answer to your question is "Yes.""

"Yes?" I shout. "You love her?"

I'm rewarded by a Kelley Kips smile that should be in a museum. It's so beautiful and rare.

As Kelley nods silently, Tabitha comes rushing over in her sleek gold dress. She looks amazing. Like a Christmas ornament.

"Kelley Kips. You're coming with me."

I feel sorry for Kelley as he's maneuvered to the center stage.

"Oh no," I tell Keston. "Kelley is going to hate this."

"What are you talking about? Kelley loves to sing."

"What the hell? I thought he was shy."

Keston snorts. "Watch."

Kes is right. With the microphone shoved in his hand, Kelley transforms. His shoulders visibly relax and fall back.

His long hair drips in his eyes. He sweeps it away with one hand while crooning a song that is so moving I lose my train of thought.

The words are in Spanish. Everyone except me knows them and sings along.

I beat my tambourine gently against my leg.

To feel part of the song.

Part of this community of happy souls who don't have much in material goods but don't feel they lack anything.

"I thought Kelley was a hermit who almost never left his home until I arrived."

Kes bows his head to look into my eyes. "That's all true. You did get my recluse of a brother to venture out. To search for *pirate treasure.*" He says the last two words with a shudder.

But . . ."

"But what?" I can't take my eyes off the tall, finger-snapping, foot-tapping man Mikah declares is St. Nicholas's national treasure.

"When he was a teenager before our dad died, Kelley was a radio star. He sang on radio shows and was the lead singer in a band."

"No way. Although I can see why he would be. He sings like an angel."

"It's true. You already know what happened at our father's funeral."

"Yeah," I murmur, my heart filling with sadness for the teenage Kelley who discovered he was not the apple of his father's eye but a lie and a secret.

After the funeral, Keston's half-brother Kelley was ignored by the islanders and disowned by Keston's family.

Kes watches his brother, a sheen in his eyes. "If it weren't for you, we'd still not be talking. I wouldn't know him."

"But you do, so let's dance."

The parang music is infectious. It makes me want to keep on twirling.

As Kes and I join other couples dancing in the middle of the beach bar, Tabitha joins Kelley's one-man show.

They sound as if they've been singing together forever.

It's not enough that she is the most beautiful woman on St. Nicholas, with her honey-colored complexion, long golden brown hair, green eyes, and athletic body.

She also has a pitch-perfect voice.

"Seriously?" I mutter when they switch from Spanish songs to the Celine Dion *Titanic* song.

Tabitha looks in our direction. We've stopped dancing. I swear she's singing "My heart will go on" to Keston as if she's Kate and he's Leo.

The bar turns silent as everyone stares at the slim woman singing about the most powerful, heartfelt emotion—lost love. When Kelley joins in, there's a collective intake of breath.

The song ends. The crowd goes crazy, clapping, stamping their feet in the sand, and whistling like they won a FIFA match.

Tabitha bows her head and waves at Keston, looking as innocent as Kate when she lets go of Leo's hand in the icy waters.

"She was great, don't you think?" Kes asks me.

"*Eh,*" I mumble. "I've heard better."

In my dreams!

They sound like that famous 1970s soul duo Mom plays all the time. Roberta Flack and Donny Hathaway.

"Nah, woman, you have to give Jack his jacket."

"Huh?"

"It means you must give someone their due. If they earned it."

"Okay, what have I earned?" I ask coquettishly.

Kes opens his mouth to say something but never gets to explain.

Because over the blenders whirring and whistles blowing, I hear a deep, familiar American voice say, "Carmela Jones, I've been looking for you."

Keston's hand grips mine. I squeeze his own tightly.

Tabitha swoops down from the makeshift stage.

"Marcus O'Brien?"

I've never been so happy to have Tabitha snatch all the attention.

"What are you doing here?" she asks.

"She knows him?" I whisper to Keston.

"They met at the hospital," he says. "When Marcus came to tell me he'd pay for my surgeries if I never talked to you again."

"What did Tabitha have to do with it?"

"She was the witness to the signed deal."

My stomach churns at the thought of those two vipers forcing Kes to sign away our future happiness so he could walk again.

"Bastards," I swear under my breath.

"Did you know he was coming?"

I bite my bottom lip. "Yes. He wants to talk about Lucy. I presume."

A strange fear races along my spine.

Marcus is smiling like he won a prize. What is he and Tabitha discussing?

"I wish you'd told me, baby. In case, I have to get ready."

"Ready for what?"

"To kick his ass."

"Hmmm. I think he has bodyguards with him."

Kes points to the loud, raucous fishermen on the other side of the bar. "I've got *them*."

I roll my eyes.

"There's not going to be an international brawl. I'll speak to him, listen to him chastise me for not telling him about Lucy, and then he'll leave. Christmas is right around the corner. I won't let Marcus derail our plans or holiday celebration."

But that's not what goes down.

"You did what?" Tabitha exclaims.

"I bought the Cocoa Reef Resort. You all are now standing on *my* property."

"But that deal isn't done. It has to go through me," Tabitha argues.

He shrugs his broad shoulders. "I spoke to the prime minister." Marcus is no slouch in the gym. Or, apparently, with island governments.

He points to Keston. "You're fired."

The crowd is too stunned to say a word.

"You can't do that," Tabitha says. "That was never part of the deal."

"Our deal is done. Thank you for your assistance."

"Wait . . . what?" For the first time ever, I see Tabitha looking unsure of herself.

He smiles tightly. A smile I know well. It always made me back down.

"You're an ass," Tabitha regroups and spits out.

The crowd gasps.

I stare in amazement. Did Tabitha St. Clair curse at Marcus O'Brien?

Even Marcus looks confused.

Tabitha flicks her hair over one shoulder and confronts him head-on, her eyes blazing.

"Keston Kips runs this entire drinks and entertainment area of the resort. Your repeat customer base is because of him. You're an ass to fire the best employee."

A voice in the crowd shouts, "You can't fire Keston. Who'd make our drinks?"

Marcus doesn't blink. He's a New Yorker used to rude backtalk.

At that moment, Dex puts a glass of *Punch de Creme* in Marcus's hand.

"Take a sip," Dex says. "You might want to reconsider."

Marcus looks at the drink as if it's poisoned. He slides it onto a nearby table. "I've made up my mind."

His gaze catches my eye. "We need to talk."

The crowd boos him.

"Did you know he was buying the Cocoa Reef Resort?" Kes asks, anger dripping in his words.

"No, I did not."

Kelley appears next to Keston. They stand together like a united front, blocking Marcus from seeing me.

I'm grateful to have not one but two protectors.

But I don't deserve them. Because I'm sure it's my fault. I caused this travesty.

Chapter Twenty-Nine

After convincing the brothers that I'd be fine alone with Marcus, I leave the pool area and walk along the pathways to a cabana for the much-dreaded conversation I need to have with my child's father.

Except Marcus doesn't walk to a cabana.

He takes a path that winds around the extensive grounds, past flowering trees and bushes, past fountains with marble fish spouting water, and past the outdoor breakfast area where you can sip coffee and stick your feet in the sea at the same time.

It's a beautiful place. Marcus will ruin it.

Already, the feeling of calm and tranquility that permeates every part of this resort has disappeared.

It's as if the resort knows it's been bought by a madman.

And not mad, as in a spontaneous, impulse buy, which I could understand. But mad, as in pissed-off revenge, which I can't.

"Did you really buy the resort?" I ask, still stunned at his announcement.

"I did. It's a good investment."

"Is that true?"

"You can review the due diligence from my legal crew."

"Just the words "due diligence" give me the shivers."

"But why a resort on St. Nicholas? You don't know anyone here. You don't even *like* anyone here."

Especially me, I think. And Keston.

He shakes his head. "Not true. I care for you a lot. Still."

"Why?"

We've walked to what seems like the other side of the resort. I usually drive a golf cart around here.

He keys open a door to a villa. "This will be my home on the island."

I follow him into a large dining room with crystal chandeliers and a massive couch the size of Keston's entire cottage.

The rugs are thick and soft under my feet. The walls are adorned with colorful paintings by local artists.

I'd have been impressed with all this luxury and opulence just a month ago.

Now, after learning to downsize and appreciate a more authentic lifestyle, I can't wait to leave.

I sit on the edge of a chair and give him my full attention.

"I'm here to listen to whatever you want to say about Lucy. But that's it."

Marcus walks to a bar and pours a drink.

"I never cared for all those fussy cocktails. What's wrong with a straight-up glass of bourbon."

"Nothing if you're a wealthy landowner in Texas."

He laughs. "Touché."

"Whatever, man. You do you. But why have you got to mess with their livelihoods?"

"I'm not messing with anyone's livelihood. Only his. He broke a promise to me. I could sue him."

I scoff. "Good luck with that in a local court."

"Exactly. My legal team dissuaded me. But then there was this." He opens his palms as if to show me the power he holds.

"All I see is air."

He barks a laugh. "I never knew you to be feisty, Carmela Jones."

"You never knew me at all."

He fixes a stern eye on me. "Whose fault is that? I loved the woman I thought you were. The one you showed me. Don't I get credit for that?"

"Love isn't about giving or receiving credit."

"Then what is love? Because it sure isn't having a child and giving her away without even attempting to find the father and getting help raising her."

The anger in his voice is understandable. I'd feel the same if it were me.

"You were on your way to being a millionaire. After our weekend hook-up, you told me you didn't have time for relationships."

"You're right. I said that. But I didn't know the circumstances."

"Fair enough," I grant him that. "I am sincerely sorry I didn't tell you. But that was only because I wasn't sure she was yours."

His eyebrows crease together. How many men were you with, Carmela Jones?"

"None of your business."

"Apparently, it was none of Lucy's either. You could have told us, whoever we all were. Tests could have been taken. The father, me, could have been discovered. Lucy could have had a different life."

Everything he's saying is true.

I stare at the swirly marble pattern on the shiny floor.

It takes all of my energy, self-esteem, and new-found belief that dwelling in the past is a major cause of unhappiness to look Marcus in the eye and say, "I am sorry for any pain I caused you. But I do not owe you anything. I hope you can build a good relationship with Lucy as I plan to do."

I can hardly believe I'm saying these words out loud.

I'm channeling Keston, my mom, and my girlfriends. They helped to shape me with their love and wisdom.

Especially Keston, who taught me that I must forgive myself.

Marcus is not impressed. "I could destroy you and your bartender's lives. Like this." He snaps his fingers.

"The real question, Marcus, is why would you want to?"

I stand up and smooth down my skirt. "I'm going now."

He shakes his head. "Why do you want this life over everything I can give you? You can't be happy here with so little. It's remote and primitive. Almost uncivilized."

My turn to laugh. "You're right. It seems exactly like how you describe it. And you haven't even seen my personal mode of transportation yet."

He looks at me quizzically. "What is it?"

I square my shoulders and say proudly. "I ride a donkey named Trixie."

His jaw drops wide open. "Get outta here."

I'm not usually a smirker. But I can feel my lips pressed tightly together, going up on one side of my face.

"I plan to. On Trixie."

The 11th day of Christmas dawns on a cloudy, rainy, sad day.

Marcus was not bluffing.

He is indeed the new owner of St. Nicholas's only resort. And Keston Kips is indeed out of a job.

The Cocoa Reef Resort is under new management. They kept all of the employees except for Keston.

Dex was offered Keston's job. He shows up at our house to tell us he quit.

"I'm not working for him. He's petty and mean," Dex says. "So what if he has a lot of money?"

Dex smacks the porch railing with all the disgust of his young twenty-year-old self.

I'm impressed with his loyalty to Keston, but he shouldn't quit a perfectly good job.

It's early Saturday morning and we're having a pow-wow on our porch.

Me, Kes, Kelley, Dex, and Tabitha. I did not invite her. As far as I'm concerned she's a traitor.

She arrived with Kelley in his brand new old truck. It looks as if it will fall apart any minute.

"That's a health hazard, dude."

He proudly tells me it is a zero-emission car in EV mode.

"Kelley converted the old fuel-burning engine to an electric one by himself," Tabitha says proudly. "The only one of its kind on St. Nicholas."

"Wow! I didn't know you were a mechanical engineer on top of everything else."

"I'm not," he says seriously. "I do what needs doing."

"Great philosophy," I admit.

"My only problem is finding places to charge it. But it's worth it for the environment."

"I have Trixie," I brag. "I don't have to plug her in at all."

Trixie brays loudly at hearing her name.

We all chuckle, except Tabitha, who looks at me as if I'm an alien.

Keston perches on the porch railing next to me. I'm cross-legged on the floor, picking brambles from Trixie's coat.

Last night, Keston and I walked her home through the woods to our home.

His property sits on its own beach but technically adjoins the Cocoa Reef Resort's own. Which makes us neighbors with Marcus. Ugh!

If you go by road, it takes a half hour donkey ride to get there. Through the woods and over the river rocks, it's only a ten to fifteen-minute trek.

"Now what?" I ask, looking around at our motley crew.

"You knew he wanted to buy the resort, and you never said anything?" Dex asks Tabitha, exactly what I wanted to ask.

All eyes are on Tabitha.

"He used me," she growls. "Marcus O'Brien told me St. Nicholas has a lot of potential. He would help the island prosper. He didn't say he was buying the Cocoa Reef Resort."

"St. Nicholas is wonderful as it is," Dex says. "We are prosperous. In our own way."

"I agree. It's not commercialized or cruise ship crazy. I love riding Trixie along the roadways, even to town."

Tabitha looks like someone stole her favorite doll. "I'm sorry everyone. I got suckered. He was interested in government property for sale on the island. Especially beaches and any smaller islands. My job as head of St. Nicholas's Property

Department was to tell him. But I never suggested the resort. He went over my head."

"I didn't know the resort was owned by St. Nicholas," I say.

"We bought it when the original owner wanted to sell it. But Marcus seemed more interested in our smaller islands. This resort sale caught me off guard."

My stomach clenches at her words. "What other islands? What island does he want to buy?"

She does not blink. "No Man's Land. He saw most of it from the helicopter when he rescued you. He says it would make a great all-inclusive resort."

"No!!" I cry, covering my face with my hands. "Not that island."

"Not *any* island," Keston growls.

We're all silent as the rain beats down on the galvanized roof, making drumming sounds.

The coconut leaves drip water like miniature waterfalls. Empty coconut shells fill up with clean rainwater. Trixie heads toward one and drinks with loud, happy noises.

Keston swings one leg, his expression glum. This is the first time I've seen him look upset.

Angry? Yes.

Sad? Yes.

Dejected? Never.

I don't think it's in his genes to feel blue. I want to remind him he's the descendant of an African prince turned Pirate King and a Scottish princess, but I refrain myself.

Everyone can have an off day. Or two.

Keston's mood matches the dark heavy clouds hanging over St. Nicholas.

He looks at our little group sadly. "I've never been fired before. I've never worked anywhere but the resort since I left school at eighteen. Cocoa Reef Resort was my home."

His misery is worse because it's Keston Kips, the man who cheers everyone up with his heartfelt wisdom and exciting cocktails.

No one says anything.

If we were in the States, people would be quick to say, "It'll be okay." And "Look on the bright side." Or even, "When one door closes, another opens."

All positive mantras, for sure.

But down here, no one sugarcoats anything,

They call it as it is.

"That sucks a big mango," Dex says. "He's one grimy man."

"You're screwed," Tabitha adds, looking at her long perfectly polished nails. "Marcus O'Brien is not going to change his mind."

She cocks her head to one side. "Unless CJ takes him back." She eyes me hopefully.

Keston snorts, "Over my dead body."

"Thank God," I whisper in Trixie's ear. "I can't see you catching the subway in New York."

Although Kelley and Keston have only recently been reunited as brothers, Kelley looks like he might cry.

"I know how it feels to lose your home," he says.

He picks up a rock and hurls it toward the beach. We're pretty far from the water, but it hits an incoming wave.

I swear he's unreal.

There's Beyoncé. Simone Biles. And Kelley Kips.

Kelley's story of loss and loneliness adds to the despair of the morning. We all know it. Even me.

I stroke Trixie's ears. Sometimes the only thing to say is nothing at all.

Chapter Thirty-One

The silence is almost unbearable. I'm trying not to think too hard. Or ask any questions. I don't want to add to Keston's stress.

But what will happen to us?

Neither one of us has a job right now.

Where will we get the cash flow to start True Love Trips? We have to pay for gas for the boat. Buy the luxury items for the picnic baskets and advertise.

The plan had been for Keston's salary to fund most of it until we started making money, and then we'd put all the profit into building the business.

But with no job, there can be no business.

At least we have a home, food, and fresh water. We are fortunate.

Maybe I should focus on helping Keston get a new job if he wants to. We have not talked about his options.

I rub my forehead where it hurts from overthinking.

On top of everything, the rain pours down harder than ever.

"Can I make tea for anyone?" I ask, heading inside the humid cottage. With the windows closed, the air is still. We only run the air conditioning at night.

Tabitha says not for her.

She pulls up the hood on her rain jacket and crosses her arms. It doesn't look as if she's leaving anytime soon.

It's taken me a while to get used to the idea that she'll always be around. It's a small island. She and Kes went to school together.

She's Keston's ex-girlfriend. But she was Kelley's only friend for years.

That last part makes me think she can't be all bad.

Inside the kitchen, I boil water and prepare a tray of mugs, a pot of tea, and a small bowl of honey. This gives me time to think.

Ideas pop in and out of my head like a merry-go-round where the horses go up and down.

When I hand out the mugs, I sit on the porch next to Trixie. I ruffle her ears.

"I have an idea," I say.

"What?" Everyone asks.

I turn to Keston.

"I could go to New York to work for a few months. My old firm would take me back. I'd save money and return for us to start our business."

It sounds so reasonable in my head.

The look of horror he gives me makes me feel as if I suggested I plug a finger into a live socket.

Tabitha smiles. "That sounds like a plan."

Keston still looks horrified. "Woman, I don't want you to leave. In fact, why are you sitting so far from me all morning? I need you. Trixie doesn't."

Trixie gives a loud, disgruntled "Hee-haw."

She stands up and shakes her entire body as if showing us her displeasure.

"Fine, you need her too," Kes says to the donkey. "But I'm number one. Don't forget that."

"Well, this is a first," Tabitha snorts. "A man and a donkey fighting over a woman."

"I have to agree with Tabitha. This is not just a first; it's ridiculous. I have enough love to go around."

I wrap my arms around Trixie's neck, and she sits back down beside me.

"Whoa, woman, where's my hug?" Keston says grouchily.

Tabitha rolls her eyes. Kelley slides his hands into his pockets and smiles to himself.

I leave my mug on the floor and wrap my arms around Keston's muscular frame. "There's more where that came from," I whisper in his ear.

He gives me his first smile of the day.

"You're not leaving. You forget I'm co-dependent on you."

I smack him lightly for making fun of the word I taught him. "I told you that wasn't a good thing."

"In America, maybe."

"Anywhere."

He squeezes his muscular arms around me tightly. Leans back and eyes me with total love and devotion in his deep brown eyes.

"We're a team. That means we don't split up when there's a problem. We huddle together and solve it."

A whoosh of love overtakes me. "Okay," I say humbly. My heartbeat slows down. It had been racing wildly at the idea of leaving him and Trixie.

Keston cradles my hands to his chest. "Say after me, 'I'm not going anywhere.'"

"I'm not going anywhere."

"For the people in the back."

"I'm not going anywhere," I raise my voice.

Dex and Kelley clap.

Tabitha mumbles under her breath.

Keston kisses me, ignoring the people in the back and all around.

I must say, I feel one hundred percent better. He's right. I should not try to solve this alone, as I did when I was preg-nant with Lucy.

A loud rumble rolls across the heavens right before a flash of lightning brightens the sky for a second. The jagged light cutting against the cloudy sky and choppy sea reminds me that I am not in charge of anything.

"You know what, guys," I say, looking around the porch. "Let's regroup and pivot."

The blank stares I get make me laugh out loud.

"It's what I would do in court when a trial wasn't going as expected."

"Does it work?" Kelley asks.

I hesitate.

For all I know, Kelley has a law degree somewhere at his farm.

I take a deep breath. "Yes, it does. When you have a good team."

Chapter Thirty-Two

After we decide to sleep on the news and come up with ideas for moving forward, our pow-wow dissolves.

Tabitha and Dex leave with Kelley in his deceptive old truck.

I pick up the teapot and mugs and head inside.

When Trixie and I return to the porch, Keston is nowhere around. The wind is blowing hard, though, and the floor and cushions are soaking wet.

My face and hair get drenched.

I skid backward, trying to open the door to the dry interior. I pull Trixie by the cowbell around her neck.

"You're coming with me."

She flicks her tail and drops of water fall into my open mouth.

"Ugh!"

I finally get us both inside the house. Trixie collapses on a knotted throw rug gifted to Keston by Kelley.

"Fine, you can stay there. But no wandering around. You know he doesn't think donkeys should be inside a home."

"Hee-haw," she says cheekily, batting her long eyelashes.

"Maybe he won't see you there," I whisper. "Make yourself small."

Trixie, totally understanding every word, pulls in her hooves and tucks her long nose under a shoulder.

"Good girl." I pat her head.

Trixie and I didn't need to worry.

Kes doesn't notice anything when he returns, soaked and peeling off his clothes.

"What were you doing?" I ask.

"Securing the boat," he says. "The waves are battering the dock."

"Oh!"

"Where did you think I was?"

I shake my head. "No idea." I lead him away from the living room and Trixie's curled-up form.

He balls up his wet clothes. "I'll hang these up later. When the rain stops."

"Sure, babe."

His naked body gleams in the fluorescent light. This man is beautiful from head to toe.

His sexy salami swings like a delicious treat. No, not a treat, a full meal. I laugh to myself.

"You're drooling," he says, walking past me and closing my mouth with a kiss.

"I was thinking of the tasty homemade fruit cakes being created in kitchens tonight."

He laughs. "Right. Who do you know is making one of those holiday treats?" He puts a hand to his mouth as if waiting for my answer.

"No one. But I heard I must have a fruit cake and a pork loin for Christmas dinner."

He swats my butt with his towel gently. "I can teach you how to make them."

Then, he disappears into the bathroom. I hear the shower running. Like he's forgotten me standing here.

Keston never walks past me naked without stopping to have a bit, or *a lot*, of fun.

He must be more depressed than I thought.

When he emerges from the shower with a towel around his waist, un-shaved, and a strained look, I realize I'm right. The usual gleam in his eyes is missing.

My heart hitches for my sweet, handsome man who lost a job he loves. Unfairly.

"Hey, you," I say, following him into the bedroom.

I kick the door closed with one foot. God, I hope that was sexy and not scary.

He tries for a smile. "Hey, babe."

"I was thinking . . . ." I slide one foot, then another slowly toward him, making up this seduction as I go.

He looks at me, concern in his eyes. "Are you limping? Did Trixie step on your foot again?"

I reach his body, still slick with a sheen of water. I press a hand on his heart, channeling my inner goddess.

"No, dodo bird, I'm trying to seduce you."

He lets out a little laugh.

"Is it working?"

"Not yet. Maybe you can do more stuff." He raises his arms above his head to give me full access to his body. His massive biceps pop out. Like a damn circus act.

I grab his towel and unwrap his body slowly, sliding my hand along his skin until I reach his ass. I give it a tweak. "Like that?"

A remnant of a smile returns to his beautiful face. "Better. Although your pinch kind of tickles."

I sigh inwardly. "How does he get me hot and wet in seconds? I can't even get his towel off without making him want to laugh.

But at least he's smiling.

I run my hands up and down his sexy chest. His manhood pings right into my navel. Now we're talking.

I should take it nice and slow. Build up to a slow burn and make him sweat.

His dark nipples harden under my touch.

What the hell? Nothing ever got accomplished with a slow burn.

I attack his nipples with my mouth.

Chapter Thirty-Three

Keston lets out a low growl as my lips tease his sensitive skin. The taste of salt lingers on my tongue as I trace circles around his nipples.

His hands find their way into my hair, pulling toward me upward, but I push away and drop to my knees.

A whoosh of air escapes him. "Baby, it's hard on that wooden floor."

It sure is, but I'm not going to complain.

Not when his cock is poking me in the eye and I can feel its precum on the tip of my tongue.

"Shhh, relax and enjoy it," I say.

His body vibrates under my touch.

My fingers trail down his abdomen, stroking the sculpted muscles.

My breath hitches with anticipation as I eye his throbbing manhood.

Keston's sharp intake of breath fuels my desire as I lean in, pressing a soft kiss to the tip before taking him fully into my mouth.

A guttural moan escapes him, his fingers tightening in my hair as he rocks his hips gently, setting a delicious pace.

The warmth of his length fills my mouth, the taste of him igniting a fire within me. I hollow my cheeks, sucking with fervor as Keston's groans grow louder, music to my ears.

As I continue to suck his cock, his breaths grow ragged. His hips buck faster. His overachiever length thrusts deeper into my throat.

His cock slips out of my mouth. I lick it slowly while stretching my mouth muscles to expand for more.

I'm going to make my man thrill with pleasure the way he does for me all the time.

I reach up, gripping his ass, guiding him back into my mouth. My lips clamp around his throbbing member, sliding up and down like a piston.

Keston's moans become louder, pleading with me not to stop.

I can feel his release nearing. I normally would pull away and finish him with my hand. But not tonight.

His hot, creamy load spurts onto my tongue, and I can't resist the temptation to swallow it whole.

Keston collapses against the bedroom door, panting heavily.

I'm still on my knees, the sweat from my body mingling with the droplets of water that still cling to his skin.

My hands move softly, slowly up and down his pulsating member, making him groan with pleasure some more.

His moans mingle with the scent of our sex.

It's an exquisite cocktail.

"Woman," he says forcefully. "You own me."

A fire ignites in my loins. He owns my pussy, that's for damn sure.

I stand, slowly pulling him towards the bed with me. The sheets are soft, the covers warm, inviting us both to escape our worries for at least one night.

I push him gently onto his back, climbing on top of him, my knees straddling his hips. As I look into his eyes, I can see the lust and longing mirroring my own.

Keston reaches up, cupping my face in his hands,

brushing his thumbs over my cheeks, tracing the outline of my lips.

He pulls me down to him and kisses me deeply.

"I love you so much, CJ. Promise you will never leave me."

"I promise," I whisper.

His hands move to pull my tee shirt over my head.

It gets stuck halfway, and he has to wrestle it off.

"I think your head got fatter," he says.

I smack him.

"Ouch woman. This is abuse."

Once I'm free of my shirt and shorts, he takes over, touching me with his callused hands.

As his skilled fingers trace the delicate skin of my stomach, tickling and teasing, I feel my body responding to his touch.

With my eyes closed I let my thoughts and concerns melt away under his probing fingers.

It's like he's waving a magic wand across my skin.

His fingers trail further down, teasing the sensitive skin of my inner thighs. He swoops me over in one movement, and now I am under him.

My heart races as I feel his breath on my most intimate area. I shiver with anticipation.

Keston looks up at me, his eyes filled with lust and passion. He slowly parts my legs, spreading them wide open for him, inviting himself into this most intimate of spaces.

I feel exposed and vulnerable but also overwhelmed with heat and anticipation.

His tongue slides down my body, leaving a trail of

wetness that ignites my nerve endings. I arch my back, feeling the exquisite sensation of his lips and tongue exploring every inch of me.

His fingers tease and stroke, sending shivers of pleasure down my spine.

With each touch, each lick, each kiss, my body responds with an intensity that is almost overwhelming. It's as if every cell in my body is awakening, coming alive to his touch. I can't help but moan, my body arching and bucking with desire, begging for more.

Keston's fingers slide inside me, exploring my depths, finding that spot that sends electricity coursing through me. He knows exactly what to do, what to touch, how to kiss, how to lick, how to make me feel alive.

My body is aflame, my senses heightened, every sensation amplified.

My moans grow louder, and my breaths shallower. I can feel the pressure building, the anticipation of release growing stronger with each passing moment.

His fingers pace faster, his tongue darts in and out of me, teasing my most sensitive spots. My body prepares to explode.

And then, when I think I can't take it anymore, he does something unexpected. He stops. His fingers slide out of me, his tongue leaves my pussy, and he looks up at me.

He knows just how close I am to the edge. He leans in and whispers, "Are you ready?"

My body trembles in response, and I nod vigorously. I can barely get the words out, but I beg, "Yes, more. I need more."

A wicked grin spreads across his face. "You didn't say please."

"Oh fuck. Please!"

He pats my clit, which is throbbing like crazy. "Much better."

My old Keston is back.

I want to grin but I'm writhing like a she-devil on the bed. "More, more. more," I beg.

Without another word, his hands and mouth converge on that one spot he discovered and knows well.

His fingers, his tongue, his lips all work in perfect harmony. I'm teetering on the edge of release.

With a deep, guttural moan, I arch my back, my muscles clenching around his fingers as a wave of pure ecstasy washes over me.

My body trembles, shaking with the force of the intense pleasure.

I shout his name over and over as the orgasm rips through my belly all the way to my toes.

Tears of relief drench my face. I didn't realize how stressed I'd been. They can't seem to stop coming.

Keston sees my tears and climbs up to kiss them away. He swipes away some with his thumb.

"Don't cry, baby. We're going to be fine. We're going to prosper and grow. Together. No one and nothing can stop us. And we're always going to rock each other's worlds. Very important."

This time it's me who asks him to promise.

He kisses my shoulder and nestles next to me, yanking up the sheets to cover us. "I promise."

My hands run through his hair, and I pull him closer, savoring the feeling of his body pressed against mine.

Any concern about our passion waning disappears. This man was made for me, and me for him.

Our lovemaking may change as we grow together, but that intensity of passion won't disappear.

I finally understand that expression, '*when you know, you know.*'

I know that Keston Kips makes me feel like the most exciting woman in the world.

He must be thinking the exact same thing because he says, "No matter how much time passes, it always feels like Day One with you. I can never get enough of you. I will always want you."

"I'll always want to suck your cock," I whisper to him.

He rolls his eyes. "Thanks."

I grin. "That's for you stopping in the middle and making me beg."

"Ah. The best part."

We snuggle down with the sound of rain pattering on the roof and the ungodly smell of Trixiue's farts coming from the living room.

"Woman, that donkey is going to ruin our sex life."

"If I'm not going anywhere, neither is she."

"Fine," he grouses. "I'll build her a donkey house on the porch."

"Pink?"

He groans. "Yes, with glitter."

I fall asleep happy, sated, and feeling like a million bucks. Nah, make that a billion.

Chapter Thirty-Four

The 10th day before Christmas gets off to a rocky start.

For one thing, it's still raining. As if the weather got the same memo we did: St. Nicholas is in a depression—a meteorological and an emotional one.

Our pow-wow has expanded to include more people.

Kelley, Tabitha, and Dex arrive as expected in Kelley's Batman truck which is what I'm calling the only electric vehicle on the island. I'm going to talk to him about building one for me and Keston after this melee is over.

"Melee" is my new favorite word, a word the islanders throw about to mean anything from a disagreement with one's boyfriend or girlfriend to what's going on now. This mess caused by Marcus firing Keston.

I've made a pot of tea and homemade scones from my favorite recipe blog. We're eating and drinking and discussing plans for the Christmas party when a roar comes from around the spit of land that separates our property from the Resort's.

"What the hell?" Keston jumps up almost stepping on Trixie's tail.

I watch in total disbelief as three fishing boats zoom up to our dock, the lead boat spinning circles before tying up.

Kes grins. "Crazy bastards."

"Do they realize it's storming out there?" I ask.

"Those guys fish in worse weather. This is nothing to them," Dex says, with pure admiration in his voice. "They have balls of steel."

I gulp. "Okay, Dex. Thanks for the visual."

Tabitha rolls her eyes. "I beg to differ. They're men with toys who can't get enough playtime."

Keston runs into the rain to greet his fishermen friends, Captain Shaq, Starr, Beast, and Redfish. They leap out of the boats and swagger up the dock.

Except they don't know they're swaggering. It's their

natural gait. Probably comes from years of standing in rocking boats reeling in fishing lines.

They're loudly cursing Marcus O'Brien and his "coup."

How do they even know the word, "coup" I wonder.

But then I hear them talking loudly about blockades, boycotts, and other battle tactics and I realize I've underestimated these men of the sea.

When the oldest fisherman, Redfish mentions Sun Tzu's *Art of War*, I reel. Who are these people?

Tabitha catches me with my mouth hanging open. "They watch a lot of YouTube."

"Right," I say, embarrassed. "My bad."

Kelley watches it all with curiosity. "They just show up and Keston doesn't mind?" he asks.

"Nah," I say, waving at the fishermen, who are carrying bottles of rum and a very large fish toward some trees.

"They bring us fish when they're heading back in from work. Sometimes Kes goes with them to pull in their nets."

Kelley nods, his eyes darting from one man to another. You can almost see his brain analyzing the scene.

"Looks like they've come to cheer up Keston," Dex says.

Despite the rain, the fishermen and Kes set up a grill under the protection of tall trees that block the rain. Next to the grill they plunk down a cooler. I count three bottles of rum, two bottles of water, and a dozen cups.

"What are they doing over there? I ask, perplexed.

Dex laughs out loud. "Their mini bar, of course."

"But why under the trees? Why don't they come over here?"

"Those are outside men," says Kelley, who clearly has

figured it out before me. "They won't be comfortable here with your teacups and teapot and cute saucers with fluffy biscuits."

"Scones," I say. "They're *scones*."

Tabitha scoffs. "Be glad they're over there and not here. Trust me. Once they start drinking and singing and complaining, you'll wish they were even farther away."

"Are they having a party?" I ask.

Kes grins. "Looks like it."

Captain Shaq swaggers up to the porch. "Morning, everyone. We would like to borrow some ice please."

How does someone "borrow" ice. You can't bring it back. But I hurry inside to fill a bucket from the ice cube trays.

On my return to the porch, I hear Captain Shaq saying, "We're never going back to the resort again. They're not getting one penny of mine."

I swallow hard when I see Starr has taken off his wet jersey and is wringing it out. I wonder if he knows he could be a model in *Men's Health* magazine with his super fit body. On the cover, too.

Beast follows suit, shaking out his jersey. I blink hard.

Thank goodness I have my own hard body man to ogle. Still...I can't get used to all these guys looking like Marvel superheroes.

The island does not have any gyms.

Just a lot of beaches, mountains, and an outdoor lifestyle.

Something I want to embrace with my new business idea. If we can still do it.

Chapter Thirty-Five

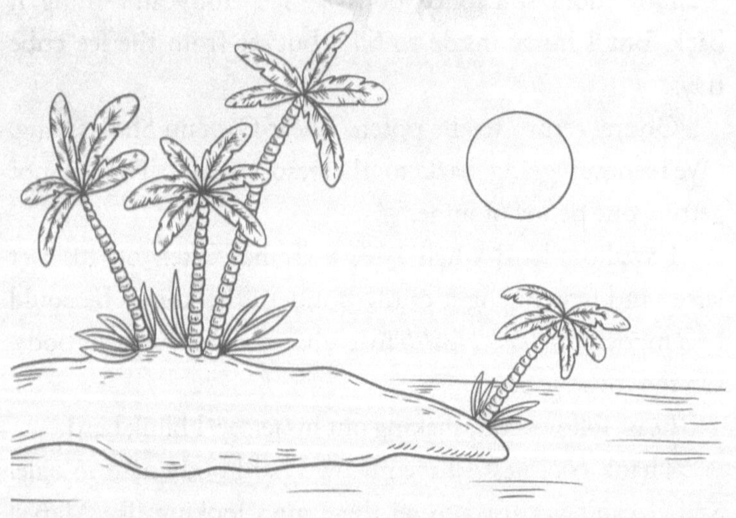

Our little tea party moves outside to join the fish grilling and rum drinking fishermen.

Kelley looks uncomfortable and sits on an overturned bucket by himself a little distance away from the group. He whittles a piece of wood he brought from his truck. Part of me wants to watch him create. The other part leans into the conversation around the smoky fire which is keeping the mosquitoes at bay.

The downpour has turned to a light drizzle. We only get wet if the breeze blows and the leaves shake off their raindrops on our heads

I accept a cup with a capful of rum.

"When in Rome," I toast the group.

The rum burns my throat. "Are you sure this isn't lethal?" I choke.

Keston pats my back. "You don't have to drink it."

Tabitha swigs her capful down in one gulp. Dex, too.

Of course I have to drink it.

I glance at Kelley. Maybe I could do what he's doing.

Kelley has sworn off rum for a while after years of carrying around a flask of his personal moonshine.

Kes and I told him he should take a break. I hid his flask.

It was a whole melee. Since then, Kelley has drunk mocktails and seems to be fine. For all I know he's created an alcohol-free drink for himself.

I hand my cup to Kes. "It's all yours. Straight rum is not my thing. I'll wait for your cocktails."

Which is the wrong thing to say. He screws up his mouth. "Whenever that will be."

"You know what the worst part is?" Dex says, interrupting Kes.

"What?" I ask.

"That jerk canceled Christmas."

"What do you mean?" I ask.

Keston's eyes narrow to slits. "No way. What about the children?"

The fishermen all speak at once.

"No way."

"What the fuck?"

"I'll kill him."

"And bury him in the sea."

Whoa. Things have turned dark fast. Maybe it's just the rum talking. Doesn't mean they'll do anything.

But my inner voice shouts, "You've underestimated them once already."

"You're not really going to kill Marcus, are you?" I whisper.

Keston pats my back. "Nobody's killing anyone."

"Yet," says Captain Shaq.

I bite my lip. They kill every day for a living. What's one billionaire to them?

Tabitha catches my eye. She shakes her head as if to say, "don't worry."

But I don't trust her. Not one bit.

Now she says to Dex. "I thought it was a nasty rumor."

Dex shakes his head sadly. "It is not. A friend who works there called me this morning. The new manager, an American Marcus O'Brien brought down to run the resort, announced it this morning at a staff meeting. He's doing away with the 'frivolous' stuff. That's how he put it."

Tabitha sighs. "Our poor kids."

Dex shakes his head. "That isn't all. He also canceled the international Christmas golf tournament. That event attracts guests from all over the world."

"Damn it," Keston snaps. "Christmas for the children *and* the tournament, which brings in revenue for the local restaurants and tour companies?"

He gets up and paces on the sand. "I was planning to enter the tournament. The prize money would help CJ and me a lot. I'm sorry, babe."

"I'm sorry, too honey. I know you practiced a lot." I turn to Dex. "Tell me about this Christmas party."

The fishermen sit quietly as Dex explains to me that every year, the Cocoa Reef Resort hosts a Christmas Eve party for all the children on the island.

"We have a Santa and presents; they can swim in the pool and play on the trampoline. The resort covers the entire cost, from food and drinks, presents for every child, a puppet show, and Santa and his elves."

"That sounds like so much fun."

"For some children, those are the only gifts they get for Christmas," Tabitha says.

"What kind of monster would cancel Christmas?" Starr asks.

"The kind we need to get rid of," Beast shouts.

"Exactly," Captain Starr slurs. "First, he cancels Keston. Then he cancels Christmas and the tournament. What's next? St. Nicholas Day?"

"He can't do that," I blurt. "He's not your prime minister. Or whomever oversees government policies."

I'm not convincing. Everyone looks worried.

Dex says. "He has a lot of money. He could probably buy the entire island."

My heart sinks to my toes, "I'll talk to him."

"Again? That could make it worse," Tabitha says. "We need a plan."

A voice of reason breaks through our pity party.

"Why don't you throw your own Christmas party for the children?" Kelley Kips says from his bucket.

He points a finger at the beach. "There's plenty of space here. If Kes and CJ don't mind the fuss. And, if you'll want, I could . . . help." His voice dies down as if he can't believe his own words.

Kelley joining a community event is like him jumping in a volcano to save everyone.

The fishermen stare at him.

"I didn't know he could talk," Captain Starr says under his breath.

'Me neither," says Starr.

Beast looks at Kelley with wide eyes. "That's a great idea. Why you sit all the way other there anyway?"

Beast, in his beastly way, staggers over to Kelley and grabs his arm. "The party is over here my brother."

Kelley blinks in shock. He stares at Beast's hand on his arm.

"Oh my," I whisper. My heart races. Kelley does not like being touched.

After a beat, Kelley says, "Thank you, Carlton." A tiny smile hovers on his lips. "You were always nice to me."

"Carlton? Seriously, that's your real name, Beast?" I'm more shocked to learn Beast is a *Carlton* than I am by Kelley's smile.

Beast looks shy. "Before I got to be a big man."

We all laugh, breaking any tension.

With Kelley seated on his bucket between me and Keston, the talk turns to how we can save Christmas for St. Nicholas.

Kelley starts throwing out his idea of a Christmas village. "My friend sent me pictures of Christmas markets in Europe. We can have our own right here. Why not?"

"Are you talking about Mikah?" I ask. "I didn't know you'll were talking like that."

He nods shyly. "We are."

He takes out his phone and fumbles with the buttons.

Then he turns it around to show us photos of the most darling wooden booths in a row, with Christmas decorations, toys, teddy bears, and food on display.

"Is that a barrel full of wine?" Beast asks in shock.

Kelley smiles at Beast. "We can do that too. But with rum."

The fishermen slap their hands together. "Let's do it."

"But who can build all that in ten days?" Dex asks. "It's a whole village of little huts. And what will Keston and CJ do with them afterwards?"

"I can make them," Kelley says seriously. "I'll make them so they can be taken apart and put back up anywhere. Like a moveable village."

We stare at him like he's nuts.

"Um . . . if I could have a little help?" he adds.

He could probably create a magical snowy Christmas wonderland in this yard by tomorrow. I don't fully understand Kelley's kind of genius. Mikah compares him to Leonardo Da Vinci, a talented artist, inventor, scientist, futurist, and way ahead of his time.

Add farmer, clothing designer, weaver, and carpenter to that, and you have Kelley Kips.

"Let's do it," Keston says. "The kids come first. We have ten days before Christmas."

Dex hums his agreement. "I'm not doing anything else right now." His dismal face makes me angry at Marcus. "I'd love to help."

The fishermen all chime in their wish to help Kelley Kips bring back Christmas to the island.

Kelley looks at each person with surprise all over his face. "Really?"

"Man, just tell us what you need us to do." Beast claps him on his back.

Kelley sticks his hands in his pocket. "Okay. I will come back tomorrow right here. CJ, thank you for the scones."

I blush. He must have heard me. "You're welcome."

"Hey, folks, we must keep it a secret," Keston says. "We don't want Marcus O'Brien or his goons to find out."

"Marcus O'Brien may have money, but St. Nicholas' islanders have community spirit, which, as I've seen, is stronger and more powerful than money," I say.

Keston rubs my back. "Thank you, sweetheart."

Don't thank me yet, I mutter to myself.

"Tabitha." I stare my nemesis in her eye. "While they

make the Christmas village, I have a plan for activities and presents for the children. Will you assist me?"

For once, she doesn't dagger me with her shark-green eyes. "I will."

You know you've reached a crossroads when you're willing to collaborate with your enemy. But it's for something bigger than myself. It's for the community.

I've been wanting to be part of St. Nicholas and this could be a way.

What is it that Ghandi says? *Be the change.*

I rub the trunk of the coconut tree next to me. It provides shelter, rain for Trixie's water bowl, a base for my clothesline to dry our clothes, and it waves to me every day.

I've named it Gang Gang Sarah, as a reminder of her mission to bring hope and healing for her people from Africa.

Now, I whisper, "Help me help your folks."

"Are you *talking* to that tree?" Tabitha asks.

I look up shocked. I didn't realize I was speaking out loud. I've gotten so used to talking to trees while stranded on No Man's Land, it seems natural to me.

The fishermen do not look fazed. I've heard them talk to the sea, the sun, the stars, and to their rum bottles.

Dex turns his finger next to his ear to indicate I'm a kook.

"Don't do that," Keston says, smacking Dex's hand.

"Sorry, man. But she was straight up having a conversation with the coconut tree."

"Kes grins. "She's nuts. But she's *my* nut. Don't make fun of her."

I beam happily at my fiancé. I knew I loved him for more than his hot body.

Chapter Thirty-Six

Before everyone takes off, Tabitha asks Keston to make us all a cocktail for the 10th day of Christmas.

"You must keep your tradition going," she encourages him. "One new cocktail for each day before the 25th."

A loud cheer of approval goes up. The fishermen especially look excited at the idea of more alcohol.

"It's five o'clock somewhere," Dex chimes in.

I stare at my phone. "It's only noon. And haven't we already been drinking rum?"

A loud chorus of *boos* shut me down.

"Make mine a mini," says Kelley. Or better yet, a mockie."

"You tell jokes now," I tease Kelley.

I realize he is much more comfortable when it's just us. And when we're in our home environment. And now his "us" has expanded to include the fishermen. I feel proud of him.

"I can whip us up some cocktails," Keston says. "And one mocktail for my boring brother. But it's not only for the 10th day of Christmas. It's to celebrate something very special."

"Like what?" Dex asks first. Followed by others with the same question.

Tabitha looks confused. Kelley is smiling like he knows.

"What in the world are you celebrating, Kes. We all want to know." My hands slap against my hips. I tap my foot impatiently.

He stares. "Did you forget?"

"Um . . . no?" I race through all the things I'm supposed to remember. Pay my bills in New York, call Mom, take Trixie to the vet for a checkup.

"Our engagement," he says disgustedly.

He picks up my hand with the gorgeous ring and shows it to me. Then, he drags me around to everyone and shows it off.

"CJ and I are engaged!"

"Oh, yeah. I forgot," I mumble.

He glares at me. Shakes his head pitifully. "I can't believe you forgot we're getting married."

"I'm sorry. A lot has happened."

The fishermen and Dex let out loud whoops and *Hell yas*. Tabitha is silent.

She forces a small smile to her face and says to Keston, "As long as you're sure. Marriage is forever."

He nods. "I'm sure."

He hops to the porch and disappears into the kitchen. I hear the blender whirling and something being chopped.

He returns with a tray of mix-matched glasses. A frothy concoction fills the glasses, topped with chunks of mango.

"You did all that in like . . . ." I check my phone clock. "Nine minutes. You are awesome."

"Thanks, babe. It's what I do." His smile flattens. "Or did."

"What's the name of this one?" I ask.

"Mango Madness."

"Yes, man, you did it again, Kes," Dex drinks his all down without stopping. "Fantastic."

Kelley swallows his in one gulp and gives it a thumbs up.

I take my time and enjoy the taste of sweet mango mixed with habanero pepper and a mysterious ingredient.

"What's in this?" Tabitha asks, swirling her glass around to collect any last drops. "Because it's magical."

I'm too busy drinking to ask questions. The mixture of sweet and spicy sensations sliding down my throat is out of this world.

I finish my delicious drink and wipe the orangey froth from my top lip. "No way you're giving up being a mixologist. It would be a travesty."

Kes's smile returns.

"Maybe I can do private events."

I wave my hand in the air.

"Didn't you always want to open your own bar?"

As soon as the words are out, I slap my hand over my mouth. He told me that in private when we were sharing secrets on No Man's Land.

Everyone turns as if in a synchronized dance to stare at Keston.

They all speak at once.

"You have to open your own bar, man," Dex jumps up excitedly. "Then you can hire me. I've learned so much from you. You won't have to do it by yourself."

"We'd come every day," Captain Shaq says, one hand over his heart. "Swear."

"Word," Starr agrees, slapping a hand over his heart in solidarity.

"You mixing, I'm drinking," Beast sings merrily.

"I can build a beach bar for you," Kelley joins in. "It can be one of the Christmas huts but larger. And more permanent."

I look at Keston expecting to see his eyes light up or a big smile or something that shows he's as thrilled with the idea of opening his own bar as we all are.

But nothing. He's staring at the bottom of his glass and frowning.

The fishermen and Dex are too busy discussing where

the best spot would be for the bar to notice Keston's lack of enthusiasm.

If Tabitha notices, she doesn't let on. Instead, she pulls out her phone. "I'm getting your paperwork ready. I can get the licensing department to issue you a temporary liquor license by Wednesday."

Keston is speechless. I suppose it's because we're planning out his life without asking if he wants to do it.

But he told me that was his dream.

I reach for his hand. "Baby, sorry to announce your secret wish. But we can do this. A bar for Christmas. I bet everyone will come here."

"You bet they will," says Dex.

Tabitha nods in agreement. "You almost *have* to do this. Where will everyone go for their Christmas cocktails now that you're no longer at the Cocoa Reef?"

I cringe inwardly.

Kelley stands up and walks to his truck. "If we're doing this, I need to get started. A beach bar *and* a Christmas market. By the way, we will need vendors and people to work in the huts. Games, food, and toys."

"I got it, Kelley, you guys work on the buildings, Tabitha and I will work on the people." I walk him to his truck. "Thank you for offering to build Keston's beach bar. We will repay you."

He stares at me, a hurt look in his eyes.

"I'm sorry. You're family. I shouldn't treat you like a worker."

"No, you should not." He slides into his old truck. "You can't pay me. I'm your family."

"Thank you," I say with my deepest sincerity. The man is right. I couldn't afford to pay him anyway.

Tabitha is standing on the other side of the truck. She hugs Keston goodbye. "It'll be okay. I promise. You'll be back making our favorite drinks in no time."

She gets in the truck and says to Kelley. "A regular bar will do, okay, nothing like a world class sculpture we'd be afraid to spill rum in."

"I'll do my best," he says.

"No," she squeaks. "*Not* your best. Do your least. Do your medium."

I giggle.

Dex follows them into the back of the truck. "See you guys tomorrow," he shouts.

I wave at his happy face.

After everyone's gone, I turn to Kes. "We're going to be very busy."

He's rooted to the same spot in complete silence.

I hope it's the good silence and not the bad kind.

I collect the glasses and wash them in the kitchen. Trixie hovers at my heels.

Every time I turn around, she's taking up a lot of space in our small home.

Since the rain has resumed falling in bucket loads, I don't kick her out.

"Can you at least hang out on the porch?"

"Hee haw," she brays, her lips stretched in a wide smile.

"Right back at you, hun," I rub her ears.

Truth is, with Keston being so quiet, I'm thankful for Trixie's clip clopping footfalls.

It's soothing and reminds me that I'm not alone.

Nobody likes to imagine their partner is unhappy with them.

Chapter Thirty-Seven

The cottage is in total darkness and it's only 3 p.m. With all the heavy rain, thunder and lightning hitting the island, the power has gone. Kes lights a few candles and puts them far from the open windows where the breeze blows in raindrops. Usually, we'd close the windows but it's too hot.

I'm drinking glass after glass of water out of nervousness because Keston is still very quiet.

Trixie is settled on the floor by the front door. The only sounds are her snores and the rain on the roof.

"When do you think the power will come back? I ask, just to say something.

"I don't know. It depends. A tree may have fallen on a power line. Or a transformer could have been hit by lightning."

"That could happen?"

I can tell he's nodding from the way the shadows on his face move in the flickering candlelight.

I am dying to ask him if everything is okay, but obviously it's not.

He's lost his job. My ex-boyfriend is wrecking his life. Because of Marcus, the St. Nicholas kids won't have their usual Christmas party. And Keston won't get a chance to compete for a large money prize in the golf tournament.

He's probably wishing he never met me.

Would Marcus even have seen St. Nicholas if it weren't for me?

No.

Would he want to ruin the place I call home now if it weren't for me?

No.

Would we be building an entire Christmas market and a beach bar outside Keston's front door if it weren't for me?

No!

I huddle into a ball on the couch and pray for light. No one tells you what it's like to be in a power outage.

Boring. Hot. Powerless, literally and figuratively.

It feels like being stranded on No Man's Land all over again.

Except on No Man's Land, we *talked*. Here, the silence is killing me.

I can't help it. I have to say something. Waiting for him to come to me is taking too damn long.

"Why do I get the feeling you're not excited to own and operate your own business?"

Maybe it's a good thing I can't see him clearly. A lot of truth can be spoken in the dark.

His hesitation now tells me a lot.

"Keston Kips, are you afraid?"

"No. It is a nice dream, but I've seen how people get running a business. They get snappy and annoyed. They worry a lot. And for what? Money?"

"That won't happen to you. You're the most carefree person I know."

"Exactly. Because I don't have much to stress about."

"You have me."

Even in the dark I can tell he's rolling his eyes. "And that's plenty."

A flash of lightning splits the night sky outside the windows. His face appears and disappears as fast. He looks so troubled. I want to go sit on his lap, kiss his brows, and tell him it'll work out.

But first I need to sit and listen to his concerns. Just as he does with me. It's funny, you can feel you have the answers for your partner. If they would only see it through your eyes.

In my opinion, having a beach bar on this very large beach property is a no brainer. Especially with Tabitha, Kelley, and Dex to help. And me, of course.

"I appreciate what you're trying to do," he says softly. "What Kelley and Tabitha and everyone is offering to do for me. I love mixing drinks. I love the idea of having my own bar to bring people together over cocktails and games. But I don't want to run a business."

"Okay." I tap my chin, thinking hard.

"How about if I run it? I can be the CEO. You can be my number one employee. You'd have to call me boss." I say with a small laugh. "I can see it now. You'd have to do anything I ask. Even . . . kiss my toes."

He grabs one of my feet in the dark and kisses it. "Done."

"Ha! But what do you think? I could handle all the logistics. You could mix drinks and be the people person."

He scrubs his hands through his curls. "I don't want you taking on more stress of a second new business. You're already planning *True Love Trips*."

Which may fail before it starts without any funding, I want to say. But I bite my lip. I'm not bringing up the word "fail."

"Do you have . . . anything else you'd like to do? Or that you *can* do?"

I realize I don't know much about Keston's skills outside of his mixologist job. I mean I know his survival skills. And his bedroom skills, but can he do anything else?

"*Hmmmm.*"

"What are you '*hmming*' about?"

"I was wondering if you have any other employable skills. Being a hot man with charm whom I adore does not count."

He sucks his teeth and stands up. His shadow moves across the wall. "I have skills, young lady."

"Oh yeah, like what?"

A beat of silence goes by. I can't tell what he's doing from my slouched position on the couch.

Suddenly, the room explodes with a hip hop song. He puts his phone down on the table.

He grabs the bottom of his shirt and gyrates to the song. He spins in a circle and rotate his hips like he's Magic Mike in a private show.

He does that wave thing with his entire torso, making his abs ripple even more.

I sit up and gasp. "What the hell?"

His shadow is moving on the wall. He's moving in front of me. It's like I have two sexy dancers for the price of one.

His broad shoulders stay still as he wines his waist going down to the floor.

"Oh my God."

He slithers and slides.

I watch mesmerized.

He pops back up and runs his hands up and down his body, flexing biceps, triceps and all his other *ceps*.

Then, his pants drop to the floor. Every inch of his majestic manhood protrudes in his shadow self.

The candle light flickers with his movements. He's dancing, gyrating, stripping, doing a full Chippendales' strip tease right here in the living room.

My man has talent. He slides up to me and swerves down to his knees running his hands feather light over my skin.

Every pore raises in anticipation of being touched.

Except he doesn't touch me. He smiles wickedly and spins off to somewhere in the dark.

Just when I think it's over, he's back. Wearing nothing but a cowboy hat.

My heart skips a thousand beats. Is this for real?

The song changes to "*Mama, don't let you babies grow up to be cowboys.*"

But it's a reggae version.

I clap my hands over my mouth as he wiggles his ass, then grabs me up and wraps my legs around his waist.

He bucks his hips over and over into my tender spot. I squeal in ecstasy.

This is the most exciting thing I've ever done with my clothes on.

I'm laughing, gasping for breath, and smacking his shoulder lightly like I'm riding my horsey.

When the song finishes, we're both breathing hard. He collapses on the couch with me still in his arms, my legs wrapped tightly around his waist.

"Well?" he asks, tilting back the cowboy hat.

"Baby," I breathe heavily. "We'll never starve. You got skills."

He laughs. My old Keston is back.
"Only problem."
"What?" he plops his cowboy hat on my head.
"You can only do that for me. And I can't pay much yet.
But I will. Trust me. I will."

Chapter Thirty-Eight

"**S**eriously, you'd be the CEO and run the bar? What about your tour business *True Love Trips*? I don't want you to give up your plans."

After his sexy dance blew off the cloud of despair hanging over us, we're sitting cuddled together hammering out ideas for our future. It's just what I'd want to do with a life partner.

I feel as if we're in this thing together, forever.

"I suggest we build up the bar here first. Then add in the tour business. That's the good thing about ideas. They can change. Or you can pivot. Besides I'm living my true love trips right now.

"And I'm the corny one?" he asks.

I laugh out loud. "You're rubbing off on me, honey."

"So, we're going to focus on the bar first? Is that what you're saying? Because that takes almost as much money to kickstart. We have to buy alcohol, remember?" He yanks a lone curl hanging in front my eyes.

"Duh! Your brother makes the best homemade wine. I'm sure Kelley can make rum too."

Kes leans back and stares at me. Even in the dark I feel the adoration in his eyes.

"Woman, we can't get a liquor license to sell *moonshine*."

"Who says they must know."

"Since when did you become such a rebel?"

"Have you tasted Kelley's dandelion wine? He makes it in different flavors. They're amazing. We could probably start our own liquor company too."

He guffaws. "Kelley won't sell his wine."

I sigh. "I know. He doesn't believe in money. But boy could I exploit his genius."

"Stick to exploiting me," Kes says, with a kiss on my nose. "Besides, I'm interested in creating experiences for people. Bringing them together to have a good time. Not in getting them wasted."

"I see your point."

He grins in my face. "But do you feel *my* point?"

I smack his arm. "Yes, my love, I *feel* your point."

"Great. Can we go back to the part where you're my boss? What else will you make me do as your number one employee?"

"If you're consenting, I can think of quite a few."

All kinds of kinky scenarios race through my mind. "Would you let me slide jelly doughnuts around your *point*? So that I can eat them and lick all the jelly?"

"What the . . . why would you want to . . . never mind . . . sure."

I snicker. Under cover of darkness, I feel empowered to say anything at all. "Would you let me squirt chocolate syrup all over your . . . ."

I don't finish because he is waving his cock in my face. It may be dark, but I can feel and taste quite fine.

"Yummy," I murmur planting my lips around his thick member.

I suck him hard, then softly, then hard again, making low moaning noises in my throat.

"I'd like to do a good job, boss," he teases, twirling my nipples between his long fingers.

My nipples harden at his touch. "You're satisfactory," I murmur.

He lowers himself to the couch his frame upside down from mine. "Let's see if I can improve my efforts."

We've never done a 69 before. In fact, in all my experience it's the one sexual position I don't favor.

Probably because I find it confusing. Like do we do it at

the same time? Or take turns? And how can I enjoy myself if I'm busy pleasing him.? Suppose I get carried away in the moment and forget about him?

I swallow my questions and force my mind to shut down.

"You're doing this," I murmur to myself.

Before I can think anymore on the topic of 69, he buries his face in my pussy and goes to town. His large tongue lashes my tender pussy lips until every bone, muscle and fiber of my body trembles with excitement.

"You know . . . ."

Screw it. I wrap my lips around his cock and take the length of him as deep as I can go. He inhales sharply.

I almost gag. I slide him out then back in, licking circles around his rosy wide tip.

Meanwhile, he's blowing rapidly on my clit with his lips puckered.

Every one of my nerve endings is exploding like fireworks.

I almost forget to suck his cock.

See! This is why I make a terrible 69 partner. I'm afraid in my excitement I may nip his tender member with my teeth.

He stops and glances over. "You okay there?" he asks politely but I can tell he's ready to do more to me. And for me to do more to him.

"I'm great."

Just concentrate CJ, you can do this.

"You know sweetheart, you're the boss," he says. "You call the shots. If you don't want to do this . . . ." He dips his head into my flowerpot and licks my petals gently. "We can stop."

"No, I don't want to stop," I breathe sharply.

He buzzes my clit with his nose, rubbing it back and forth across my tingling nub. Meanwhile I haven't been able to concentrate on his cock. I'm failing 69!

Just relax, CJ, how hard is it to do two things at once?

I lower my mouth to pleasure him. I'll try to focus on what's in front of my face. Literally.

But how can I when my entire body feels like it's on the verge of breaking into a million pieces. His tongue slides up and down my crease. His fingers move in tantalizing circles at my orifice. His breath is hot on my clit.

"Fuck, I'm going to explode."

I grab his cock like it's a gear shifter I slid into Park.

He rubs, he sucks, he licks it as if my pussy is dinner and dessert wrapped up in one.

"You're getting a promotion," I squeal.

"All I want is this," he growls, lifting my hips closer to his mouth and burying himself into my soaking wet center.

My clit trembles. I give up all pretense of doing 69 and close my eyes.

Nothing has ever felt so good or so right in my life.

I shriek with ecstasy as Keston Kips flies me over the moon. My orgasm rips through my body, mind, and soul.

He doesn't stop attending to me.

Sweet Jesus, is he for real?

My legs shake as he laps up my sweet bowl of honey like a hungry man with his first meal.

I throw my arms out and sigh.

"That was amazing," I say.

He lowers my butt to the furniture. "Did I hear you say

something about a promotion?" he laughs. "Cause all I got was a raise."

He points at his dick standing straight up.

I have the nerve to giggle. "Just give me a moment to recover."

He snorts. "I don't know, boss. It looks like you're sleeping on the job."

Chapter Thirty-Nine

All the businesses on St. Nicholas are family-owned. There are no fast-food establishments, no big box stores, or chains.

Every day, fishermen in the villages around the island return with their catch. People wait at the jetties to buy the fresh fish. Hotels and restaurants have their large coolers on standby to purchase the freshest and largest of the catch.

But whatever's not sold gets grilled by the fishermen. Or made into a giant pot of fish broth, which is more like a fish stew.

Anyone can show up and eat. Because the unique thing about St. Nicholas, despite its sporadic cruise ships, its newly expanding airport, and its luxurious Cocoa Reef Resort, is that it's still a "share everything" village culture.

That's my word for it. "Share everything."

The first time Keston and I rode around the island on his motorbike, he stopped at a few of these villages. I was shocked that we didn't have to pay to eat the grilled fish.

You could buy the fishermen a beer or a glass of rum to say thank you. But you didn't have to.

The share everything culture doesn't always work in your favor though. Keston explained that people share everything from their bikes to their weed wackers. Even soccer cleats if necessary.

"Share means share." He'd smiled at me. "Except of course I'm not sharing you!"

"I should hope not."

But I was puzzled. "Even if I pay a lot of money to ship a brand-new kayak here, (which I was thinking of doing), I still have to share it?"

He nodded. "Yup."

It was a sobering thought. The share everything culture sounds ideal in theory. But it's something I'd have to get used to.

Or be banned from eating fresh fish for free.

"It works," Keston said soothingly. "If we need help with anything, building a home, fixing a boat, or just eating a meal, the villagers will pitch in. You give them something to drink as a thank you."

"Oh," I'd nodded. "Okay."

That conversation occurred during my first week here.

Now, I'm watching the share everything way of life unfolding in our front yard.

I finally get it. These folks don't play.

We wake each morning to the sound of Kelley's truck pulling up to the house and Trixie trotting over to greet him, as if she's a dog and not a semi-wild donkey.

Each day, Kelley brings pre-cut, sanded, and painted pieces of wood to build the Christmas market huts.

Keston, Kelley, and Dex work hard all morning setting up the seven Christmas huts and Keston's beach bar.

The bar looks like something you'd find on a Pinterest board of Best Beach Bars.

Kelley can't go small or basic at all.

The fishermen arrive in the afternoons after they finish cleaning their catch and selling it.

They bring a cooler of beers, a portable radio that blares songs like, *Santa Looking for a Wife in the Caribbean*, and their jolly, positive attitudes.

They take turns helping, drinking, dancing, and snoozing.

In the spirt of Christmas, I baked cookies, scones, cupcakes and even a mango pie. They devoured everything in under ten minutes on the first day.

Now I just stay on the porch and observe.

"I swear your man doesn't sleep," I tell Mikah on video call the week before Christmas. I point the phone camera at Kelley, who is sawing wood shirtless, his tatted body gleaming with sweat.

Thankfully, they're building it hundreds of yards away, so the noise of construction doesn't bother me as I work on my laptop to make flyers for the St. Nicholas Eve party.

I'll have to go into town to make the copies at the library and start passing the flyers around. With how fast news travel on this small island, I'd bet most people already know about it. Even Marcus at the Cocoa Reef Resort must know.

"He's not my man," Mikah sighs.

"*Sheesh*," I say. "You can get any man you want, girl."

That's no lie. She's a sexy super model, although we've recently found out that her supermodel status is a front for her clandestine work as a spy. But still . . . *super model*! Hello!

"I can't *get* Kelley Kips. He's more elusive than an arms dealer pretending to be a legit CEO."

"Whatever that means," says Giselle. She's slurping a coffee from each hand before starting her day as a principal of her middle school.

"Caffeine much?" Lisa, our brainy astrophysicist friend remarks.

"Damn right. It's Christmas season, you'll know what that means?" Giselle grouches.

"We do," I say soothingly. "You have the Christmas pageant and tests, teacher evaluations and report cards."

"Right," Giselle sighs. "You forgot mean parents threatening me if I don't put their little one as the lead in the school Christmas pageant. I'd give anything to be building a Christmas market on an island instead."

"Me, too. I'd give anything to be rubbing Kelley's body with suntan lotion," Katana says. "He's yummy."

"Girl, keep your eyes on your husband and children and leave my man alone." Mikah says.

"He's not your man," Katana argues. "You just admitted."

"I don't think he's ever going to be," Mikah says sadly. "I'm used to men blowing up my phone, begging to see me."

"He's not the thirsty type," I say. "But he did mention he was interested in taking a special someone on my first *True Love Trips.*"

As much as it's killing me not to squeal, I don't want to tell her he said he loved her. I think he should tell her that himself.

"Who is it?" they shout.

"I don't know. It's probably you, Mikah."

"Girl, find out."

"I asked but he didn't say."

"Did you start the company already?"

"No, we're going to work on Keston's bar first." I explain the plan to my friends.

They *ohhh* and *ahhh.*

"Imagine having your own beach bar on your own

beach," Giselle says. "Girl, I'm happy for you. You're living the life."

I don't tell them we're penniless.

"We couldn't do any of it, not the bar or the Christmas market for the kids, without the help of everyone we know. The fishermen are arriving as soon as they return from the sea. They spend the rest of the day here working. One of them is laying pathways lined with seashells all around the huts. Kind of a maze for the children to follow. It's beautiful."

"Take photos of your progress,' Lisa says.

"She means take photos of all those hot men shirtless," Katana cackles.

I laugh along with my silly girlfriends who I miss terribly. "Mikah, when do you arrive for the holidays?" I ask.

"December 23rd. In time for your party."

"Awesome, anyone else wants to visit? Only problem is I'll have to find rooms in a guest house as we're never going back to Cocoa Reef Resort now that Marcus is running it."

"You mean ruining it," Giselle says. "I can't believe he fired Keston. How petty."

I'm silent thinking about how much Marcus O'Brien has affected my life. From being Lucy's father to my boyfriend of five years, to now infiltrating my new island home.

"Maybe he wants you back," Lisa says.

"He definitely wants her back," says Katana. "She's the only woman who doesn't care about his money."

"I could use some of it right about now, though," I joke.

"Can you show me Kelley one more time before we hang up?" Mikah asks. "I miss him."

I turn my phone around and scan the yard. Keston is lugging tree branches for the roofs. Kelley is directing him. Dex is hammering. Trixie is hanging about trying to help.

"These guys don't play around," Giselle says. "Those huts are going up quickly."

I walk over to them. "Hey, guys, say hello to my friends."

They look up sweaty and flustered. Kelley stops and wipes the sweat from his brow. I hear Mikah panting from here.

Keston smiles and waves. Dex throws a kiss.

"I'm packing my bags," Mikah groans. "Keep him single for me please."

'I'll do my best."

After I hang up, I call Tabitha. We've been coordinating decorations and presents for the kids. She has single handedly gone around to all the shopkeepers and store owners to get donations of games, toys, and sports equipment. Many have also donated cash to help with the food and drinks.

I must admit that woman can hustle. She showed up yesterday with a giant bag of toys that made me want to cry.

"Everyone is so generous," I told her.

She'd looked at me strangely "Everyone looks out for everyone."

I'd nodded silently. Marcus may try to ruin Christmas,

but he doesn't know that the St. Nicholas' Islanders community spirit can't be broken.

My job is to promote the event and organize the activities for the children, including a Santa.

The usual Santa is a Cocoa Reef Resort Food Manager who does not want to jeopardize his job by fraternizing with the enemy. So, basically, I'm on a Santa search.

All ideas of finding a traditional chubby, round faced, white-bearded Santa has been scrapped.

I've been thinking . . . *maybe* to recruit Beast. He's tall, muscular, and with an angular face, all non-Santa features – but Beast is the jolliest of the men.

If he agrees, I'd have to find him a Santa suit to fit. A six foot, four-inch-tall Santa suit.

I can't ask Kelley to do one more thing! I must figure this one out by myself.

"Guess what?" Keston beams on the 7th day before Christmas. He's waving a large brown envelope above his head after roaring up on his motor bike.

"What?" Dex asks.

Kelley stares intently at Kes's rusty motorbike. Probably figuring out how to convert it to a quiet EV one.

"Tell me you found a Santa," I put two hands together in praying mode. I hurry down the steps to join the guys.

"Nope. Good luck with finding yourself a Santa." He winks playfully.

"You do realize that Santa is the most important part of our St. Nicholas Eve party?" I snap.

All three men turn eyes at me.

I bite my lip.

"I mean . . .um . . . the Christmas village is very important too." I wave my hand feebly in the direction of all their hard, back breaking work.

Keston grins. "We know what you meant."

"Just tell us your news. Sorry I brought up Santa," I say grouchily.

"Tabitha did it." He waves his brown envelope again. "You are now looking at the newly licensed owner of our beach bar business called . . . ."

He looks at me. His grin grows wider. Damn. Can this man stop *being* so cheerful? I have a lot to do and so little time.

"What?" I ask, exasperatedly.

He takes one of my hands. "*Lucy in the Sky.*"

A river of love floods my heart. I'm speechless. Keston Kips has done it again.

"*Lucy's* for short," he says. "What do you think?

"*Lucy's?*" I whisper.

He nods. "I want this to be ours. My new family. You, me, and Lucy your daughter who I can't wait to meet. But most of all a reminder of the first day we met. And all we've been through."

"It's perfect," I whisper. "Thank you."

I could never forget Keston pretending to mistake me for the star in the sky named Lucy, composed entirely of diamonds, because of my glittery dress.

"I hope your Lucy comes to visit us soon."

"I'll tell her," I say.

Lucy and I text each other every couple of days while she studies for her final exams. As much as I want to steal her away to St. Nicholas for Christmas, I respect . . . no, I'm *thankful* she has a loving family to be with over the holidays.

"Okay," Dex claps his hands. "Let's finish this hut then we can take a proper break for fifteen minutes."

Dex has shown himself to be a talented project manager on our work site. I'll speak to him afterwards about taking online courses and getting certified.

I hustle my butt back to the porch. Trixie is on standby to help move things. I pat her furry ears. "You're doing a great job, girl."

She brays loudly.

I hand her an extra carrot for her troubles.

Now that we have a name for the beach bar, I open back up the web site I've started designing with a lot of help from YouTube videos.

But I can't concentrate. My heart races at knowing we only have seven, actually *six* days, before Christmas Eve and there's still a lot to accomplish.

I stare at my laptop screen. It's not helping that my calendar glares back at me.

"Fine!"

I close the laptop. I'm accustomed to getting things done online. But on St. Nicholas, most things are done in person. It's time to visit the library and see Mrs. Harris.

She can make copies of the flyer. She'll know where or how I can get hold of a Santa suit. And she can help me with an activity I have in mind for the children. One that may make this the best Christmas party ever.

Chapter Forty-One

I pedal Keston's old red bicycle up and down the winding roads to Skye Harbor, the main town on St. Nicholas. I pumped up the tires by myself because I didn't want to bother the men.

Trixie was busy helping them drag half-built huts to the intended locations. So, I'm on my own.

People toot their horns or wave hello as they whizz by in their cars or scooters.

A few men with pickup trucks slow down and ask if I need a ride. They seem genuinely concerned about all my huffing and puffing over hills and valleys, but I don't know them.

"No thank you." I give a friendly nod.

You can take me out of New York, but you can't take the paranoid, suspicious New Yorker out of me.

St. Nicholas is surprising in more ways than one. I thought it was just a vacation spot, but I'm realizing there's a lot of stuff going on behind the scenes.

Aside from wild donkeys who like to play dress up, there's hidden pirate treasure, a blue zone for living a long and healthy life, and inhabitants whose connections to their ancestors are closer than I could ever imagine.

My smile dims a little as I soar down the last hill into Skye Harbor. I'm not sure what to expect from Mrs. Harris.

I haven't seen her since I learned about her affair with Keston's father thirty three years ago.

From what I can piece together, Mrs. Harris and Kellum Kips, were bent on finding the Kipson pirate treasure. She, the island's historian, and he, the swashbuckling adventurer in search of his ancestor's riches.

They did not find the treasure. Instead, they created Kelley Kips, who Mikah says is the *real* treasure of St. Nicholas. Just everyone's too blind to see what's in front of their faces.

I agree with her there. But that's human nature.

As a mother who gave up her daughter at birth, I cannot judge Mrs. Harris for giving Kelley to his grandfather to raise in the farthest corner of the island.

Why they are still estranged, however, is a mystery to me. When I met Kelley, he was estranged from everyone. A bonafide hermit. Not necessarily by choice. It was as if the entire island decided it was better if he didn't exist.

Except for Tabitha. Who never gave up on him. That's the reason I accept her as part of our friend group.

I hope I don't let it slip to Mrs. Harris that I may know where the treasure is. It's our secret. Me, Keston, Kelley and Tabitha's. We haven't *seen* the treasure so we can't say for sure, but we believe we found its location. Which is heavily guarded by a bunch of monster moray eels, so we're leaving it alone.

No need for anyone else to die seeking a pile of gold and jewels. That's what we've all agreed on anyway. It's a secret we're taking to our graves.

My concern is that if Mrs. Harris ostracized her own son over a treasure hunt, what would she do to little old me? A foreigner with no relation to any St. Nicholas Islander. Yet.

By the time I arrive in Skye Harbor, a faint moon is rising as the sun dips westward over the hills. It's barely past four in the afternoon.

Cruise ship tourists hurry back from their excursions, bargaining for souvenirs with vendors on the waterfront.

I buy a sweet mango ice from the snow cone man and hustle out of the way as tourists bum-rush me from behind. It's like last call at the bar.

I push the bike with one hand and lick my fast-melting ice. So delicious. I need to learn how to make more mango-based dishes. Our yard is littered with mangoes that Trixie likes to chomp on.

When I turn the corner into Old Town, I breathe a sigh of relief. I finish my ice and jump back on the bike.

Pedaling over the cobblestone road is no fun.

I bump along, my teeth clacking together with every rotation of my pedals. When I can't take it anymore, I hop off and push the bike until I arrive at the cute blue shop called *This Place*, where Keston first bought us bottles of water and bags of almonds.

I lean my bike against the blue wall, plop down on a chair, and pant out my order.

"One double cappuccino and a croissant, please, Roberto."

He smiles. "One moment."

It's the same thing I ordered every day when I volunteered at the library and museum.

A small floral plate and teacup are placed before me. Roberto pours out tea from a teapot of lemon grass tea and places sliced limes on a plate next to my drink.

I sigh. "I'll keep dreaming, Roberto."

"One day we'll have a cappuccino machine, Ms. CJ. I promise."

"I'll wait," I smile at him.

Roberto is Keston's age, early thirties. His family owns *This Place* and Maria, his mother, is the baker.

The croissant may be a figment of my imagination, but

not the small round meat pie that arrives fresh from the oven. Flaky and moist and tasting better than a croissant.

"Thanks," I mumble as I push the entire mini pie into my mouth. It's so good.

"You going to the library again?" Roberto asks.

I nod yes because my mouth is too full to speak.

"I'll pack up the usual?" Roberto asks before turning to welcome the last wave of tourists who are peeking into his café.

"Yes, please." I swallow my mouthful of deliciousness.

Roberto knows I crave his mother's lightly fried "bakes" filled with the hard fruity sheep cheese made at a dairy across the island.

My backpack swells with the takeaway bag inside. Enough to share with Kes and Trixie later.

Now I'm fortified and ready to face Mrs. Harris.

Chapter Forty-Two

"Good afternoon, Carmela Jones," Mrs. Harris greets me warmly as I enter the air-conditioned building. "You just caught me. I was heading out soon."

Mrs. Gloria Harris, the sixty-something, former high

school principal, now librarian and museum curator, has light skin like Kelley. Her golden dreadlocks are wound so high around her head they form a crown.

If the Queen of the Island had a face, it would be Mrs. Harris. Her ancestors go back about eight generations.

Which is why her power and authority are well-earned. She's rooted in St. Nicholas. No one can deny her existence or imply she doesn't belong here.

The first time I came to town with Keston, he brought me to the library/museum because of my love for books. Within a minute of meeting me, Mrs. Harris pushed Keston out the front door and whisked me down a rickety flight of stairs to the "holding area."

She showed me how to sort through and catalog boxes of historical artifacts that had been delivered from estates around the island.

I did a good job because Mrs. Harris asked me to return the rest of the week. She said it was the only way I would learn the "truth" about St. Nicholas Island, making it seems as if there were secrets to be discovered. Which there were!

As a sucker for books and anything remotely mysterious, I agreed. A volunteer position was perfect to fill my time. Even if I felt that Mrs. Harris had an ulterior motive.

Now, I need *her* help.

Except she has her own idea for why I'm here.

"Here's the list, Carmela. I wondered when you'd be coming by to help set up the book club."

Before I can say a word, she continues, "I want to start hosting it on Monday evenings. With the island's elders. Most are retired lawyers, a doctor, a vet, and former politicians. The elite inner circle. Not to mention you must be over forty. You can host it, choose the books for me to order, and run the club."

Way to make me feel like an "elder" Mrs. Harris. Is this a dig on my being engaged to a man eight years younger than me? Or something else?

I'm just about to accept her assignment when I remember why I'm here.

The kids.

And who I am?

Carmela Jones, Esq.

I have dealt with bossy law partners, presumptuous judges, and a lot of entitled clients. I can deal with Mrs. Harris.

"Uh . . . I'm here for something else. Perhaps we can discuss your book club after Christmas."

Now it's Mrs. Harris who didn't expect this. She takes a step backward. Her eyes travel up and down my sweaty tee shirt, disheveled hair, and lack of makeup.

I cringe. I've come a long way since I first arrived on the island with my designer clothes and sexy sandals.

But I refuse to retreat. "I sent you an email an hour ago with a flyer to print. Did you get it?"

"No. I shut down the computers a while ago."

"Oh." My heart sinks. I shouldn't have stopped for a snack.

But Mrs. Harris seems to be waiting for something. My heart beats extra fast. I know that look.

The imperious "I'm-waiting-for-you-to-acknowledge-me-and-beg-for-my-help" look.

The only other place I know that can print my flyer is the Cocoa Reef Resort. It's either Marcus or Mrs. Harris.

Is there really a choice here?

I swallow hard. "I know how much you do for the people of St. Nicholas, Mrs. Harris. Your work on preserving their heritage is unparallel. Which is why I've come to request your help. It's for the children."

She raises two perfect eyebrows. Can she smell bullshit?

A smile breaks across her red lip sticked lips.

"Thank you, Carmela, that's sweet. How can I help?"

I explain about the St. Nicholas Eve party we're hosting at Keston's property.

"He's having a party? On his land?"

I frown. Why is there a glint in her eyes?

"Yes, we are. It's for the children. Since Cocoa Reef Resort canceled the Christmas party this year. I need the flyer to pass out to everyone. We want to invite all the children of the island. And their parents, too."

I'm suddenly hit by the reality of what we're trying to do. Are we crazy? That's a lot of people. It'll be like the St. Nicholas Day festival. But at our house!

I need to sit. I grasp the back of a chair and pull it out, sinking down as calmly as possible.

Don't show your weakness, I mutter to myself.

She's staring. I can almost see her brain spinning with questions.

Before she can throw any at me, I look around the darkening room. "I'd also like to borrow some of your children's books please. I plan on having a reading hut, with comfy mats on the sand. Someone will do a story time throughout the event."

Someone. Ha! Most likely it'll be me.

Mrs. Harris scowls. "Children don't read anymore. They never come in here."

I had noticed the library was usually empty.

"You could make it more exciting," I suggest.

Mrs. Harris blinks. "This isn't an *arcade*."

My hands wrap around my waist. I'd better keep my ideas to myself.

"What else are you planning for the children's activities?"

I pivot quickly. Turn up my smile and act as if entertaining over one hundred children is easy peasy.

"A sandcastle contest. A crab race. Maybe a rock skipping tournament. I almost say, "if I can get Kelley Kips to do a demonstration," but bite my tongue in time.

"My son Kelley is helping you out," she doesn't ask me, she tells me.

"Yes, ma'am."

She turns abruptly. "Go ahead and choose the books you would like to borrow. I will print the flyer."

Damn, if I'd known that mentioning Kelley would light a fire under her, I'd have shouted it as soon as I entered the room.

"Thank you," I say releasing a breath. "I'll make a pile of books and have Tabitha stop by tomorrow to pick them up."

She stops and turns slowly.

Oh oh.

"My niece, Tabitha St. Clair, is involved?" She mutters something under her breath.

I can't detect the tone in her voice. Is it possible I'm not the only person on St. Nicholas who doesn't love the tall, golden beauty?

But I can't throw Tabitha under a bus she doesn't see coming. I give Jack his jacket. "She's been very helpful."

"Hmmmm," Mrs. Harris murmurs as I hold my breath. I really need to keep my mouth shut until I understand these complicated family dynamics. I grew up in a small town in upstate New York, but this is an island. They share everything; except their deepest secrets.

Chapter Forty-Three

The prickly feeling overtaking my body reminds me of my mother's favorite line from Shakespeare's *Macbeth*; "Look like the innocent flower, but be the serpent under it."

In this case, the serpent disguised as a flower would be

Mrs. Harris. For all I know she's the one who arranged to have those horrible sea serpents guard the treasure to deter anyone else from finding it.

She may have gotten Kellum Kips killed. Not on purpose, but by accident.

His death is a mystery to everyone. His body was never found. But someone has to know something.

Years of being a trial lawyer has taught me that everyone believes they are the hero of the story.

And if you probe a needle into the tiny stitches of their narrative, if you unravel the smallest details that do not seem important at all, eventually the entire fabric falls apart.

Then Wham! The truth is laid bare.

But don't waste your time pointing a mirror at them hoping they see the truth in their reflections.

The only thing that pointing out flaws does is build resentment.

Which is why I don't mention Kelly, her amazing son. Or Tabitha. Or even Keston.

I'm going to focus on the flower, because eventually the serpent will slink out from under the petals all on its own.

"Thank you so much, Mrs. Harris," I swoon for real when she returns with a folder of my lovely flyers. "I don't know what I'd do if you weren't here."

Which is true.

She gives a tight smile.

"Look what I've found!" I pat the pile of picture books I think the kids will enjoy.

She scans them out and hands the pile back. "Good selection," she says grudgingly.

I smile and pretend I'm clueless as she smooths down her dress.

"What else are you planning?" Mrs. Harris rubs her temple.

I invented that move. Pretend you have a headache while digging for information.

"We're trying to get *The Mangoes* to perform."

Her lips turn up. "Good luck."

"Thanks."

"Is there anything else I can do?" she asks.

I look around the empty library.

Then it hits me. There's no serpent. She wants to be invited. But doesn't have any children to use as an excuse to attend.

Maybe . . . and this could be my wishful thing, Mrs. Harris has been looking for a reason to connect with Kelley. And is too proud to make the first move. Or doesn't know how.

A thought at the back of my head probes at my own tiny stitches in my own hero story. . . and unravels it.

Maybe's she's scared. Like I was. She could have imposter syndrome too.

I straighten up. Look her in the eye. I speak to her as one birth mother to another. As a woman who gave up a child and seeks to reconnect.

"Please come. We will have something for everyone. Not just the kids. I'm planning a pirate theme scavenger hunt I could use your help with." I make that up on the fly.

"Really?" she perks up.

"Yes." I spread my hands enthusiastically, already imagining the reunion between mother and son that I'm orchestrating in my head.

"Everyone loved the Pirate regatta's scavenger hunt, right?" I ask. "We can create a Christmas themed pirate one."

I haven't forgotten the mad dash through the waters of St. Nicholas on the hunt for items like a shell from Mermaid Pool. And the all-nighter party on the beach afterwards.

She nods. "It's our annual tradition."

"What if instead of a list of random items we organize it as a real-life pirate treasure hunt? With real clues? And people will have to read chapters from an old diary, and study historical documents like those you have here." I swing my arm out to encompass the old maps on the walls.

"A real-life pirate treasure hunt," she muses. "With real-life historical documents?"

"Yes!" I clap my hands, getting pumped. "That way more folks, both locals and tourists, will be interested in the museum. And encourage reading. You'll be flooded with visitors. Once we spread the word about St. Nicholas's pirates. Especially the Black Pirate King."

As the idea forms in my head, I see the beauty of it. Connecting the past to the present will showcase what the island has to offer besides its beaches and waterfalls. Like its history. It's culture of sharing. In this case, knowledge, and hopefully wealth.

Light glints from Mrs. Harris glasses. "You found it," she whispers so low I barely hear her.

"Excuse me?"

"You know about the Black Pirate King," she whispers.

"Nuh uh," I deny outright.

"You know where the Kipson's treasure is." The emotions on her face are warring with each other. A mix of admiration and anger. Can someone look admiringly angry?

I can't see myself, but I feel all the blood in my face draining away. I must be as pale as the ghost of Charlotte Campbell.

"Um . . . it's an island myth, isn't it? Everyone knows."

The side of her mouth tilts up. It's not a smile. It's pure skepticism.

If I thought I was reading Mrs. Harris correctly as a woman interested in meeting her son, I was deluded.

Her eyes are bright as stars behind her glasses. Her hands squeeze themselves into fists. Her regal persona fills with new-found energy. And not the positive kind.

"You found it." Mrs. Harris slams her palms down on her wooden desk. "I knew that bitch had something up her sleeve. Something she wasn't sharing with us."

I'm in shock at the venom I hear in Mrs. Harris's tone.

My serpent theory reemerges.

She must sense my distress because she blinks the fire from her eyes and softens her voice. Or tries to.

"I've asked Viola Kips for years if she had anything in her possession about the St. Nicholas Island treasure. She denied it. When she passed away three years ago, I expected she would leave her historical documents to the museum. Then I could find it myself.

"But she didn't," I say softly, backing up to the door. I'm in a dark library with a mad woman.

She's fast for a woman in heels. She blocks the front door.

"Viola Kips left everything to her grandson Keston."

Not everything, I want to say but bite my tongue. I'm not telling her about what she left for her other grandson, Kelley. Mrs. Harris's own son.

"Everyone knows her son, Kellum Kips, had inside information about the location of the pirate treasure and wasn't telling anyone. But we all assumed the information died along with him. Except for me. I knew if he had any insider knowledge he got it from his mother. Shoot, it was Viola who encouraged his dangerous obsession. Poor Kellum. It ruined his marriage and his relationship with Keston."

I gulp. She's clearly delusional. She's forgotten her affair with Kellum Kips. Was Mrs. Harris in love with the man who fathered the Kips boys?

Or was it a case of the heart wants what the heart wants, and in her case her heart wanted the Kipson pirate treasure.

"The treasure belongs to all of us. Every St. Nicholas Islander suffered the same history of slavery and colonialism, and we all deserve a piece of the treasure."

A light bulb goes on over my head. Is this where the share-everything theory originated? In their shared history? It makes sense.

"I see your point, Mrs. Harris." I inch toward the front door.

She crosses her arms over her very large chest. She looks formidable. Focused and unmoving.

Keston was right. Treasure hunting is like an addiction.

My heart races.

She's not really threatening me, is she?

She's a librarian for God's sake. What will she do? Beat me with a book?

I think fast. I never asked Keston about his father. I thought it was too painful to think about him being lost at sea. But maybe there were other reasons Keston didn't talk about his dad.

Was he murdered? Or disgraced? Or . . . I don't know . . . deceived by the sea witch, Mrs. Harris?

A warning thought flashes like a neon sign in my head.

"Mrs. Harris, why did you ask me to catalog important historical

artifacts at this museum the first day you met me? You didn't even know me?"

She shrugs as if it's no big deal. Then rattles off everything she knows about me on her fingers.

"You're a lawyer from New York. Your mother is Professor Jones at a prestigious college in upstate New York. Your ex-boyfriend is the billionaire, Marcus O'Brien. And you're dating Cocoa Reef Resort's bartender . . . ."

"Mixologist," I correct her. "And he's no longer working there."

" . . . . Keston Kips of the Kipson family estate."

I arch an eyebrow her way. "The last part is the most important, isn't it?"

She has the nerve to blush.

"Wow! This is a really small island." I mutter.

"Tiny," she laughs in a forced manner. "Teeny tiny. I had children's parents who called me before the school day ended because they'd already heard what trouble their offspring had gotten into."

"I thought *I* came from a small town."

"Get used to having everyone know all your business. Be careful what you say and to whom."

"I will." Starting from right now. But I keep that to myself.

"The most important reason I drafted you to help me is because you survived being stranded on an island in gale force winds. You obviously have a lot of grit and determination. Which means you won't give up."

"Thanks?"

"But that was months ago. I've been waiting for you to find something of historical value in Viola's boxes and come talk to me about it." She all but rubs her hands together like a master manipulator.

Bile simmers in my stomach.

"How'd you know I would come talk to you? *If* I found something."

"Who else would you talk to?" She opens both hands. "I know the history. I have the maps," she points to the walls. "And I have the key."

"What key?"

"Ah! You don't know as much you thought you did."

She's bluffing. I've seen this tactic a lot. I do this myself. Assume facts not in evidence to get the witness to talk.

It doesn't always work.

"Objection," I shout.

"What?"

"Nothing," I mutter.

Never have I felt more like a pawn in a game I don't

understand. And never have I felt such a strong desire to keep my mouth shut.

"Well?" Mrs. Harris's eyes are glittery and sharp. "Do you have any information to share with me? Any questions you want to ask?"

I fake a smile I use for hostile witnesses in the courtroom. "No questions, ma'am. Thank you."

Chapter Forty-Four

As I ride the bike through the cobblestone streets and toward the waterfront, I mull over the conversation.

The last thing I want to do is make Mrs. Harris out to be a villain. A villain is a victim under different circumstances.

And vice versa. I'm sure Shakespeare said something to that effect. Only with more flowery language.

I'm so wrapped up in my thoughts I don't notice the large SUV until it swings in front of me. The gigantic bumper hits my front tire.

There's nothing I can do to stop the bike flying out from under me. I land on my left foot and fall backwards.

I scream loudly. More in fear than pain. "Watch where you're going!"

The SUV screeches to a halt. There are no other cars or people around.

The vendors have packed up and gone. The cruise ship blows its horn and is pulling away from the dock. The school kids have all gone home.

The SUV is the shiniest, most tricked out vehicle to drive on St. Nicholas's pot holed roads. The color is a bright Stop sign red. The rims look like they were hijacked from Dominic Toretto. And the metal bumpers gleam like an ice rink.

I try to stand up.

"Ouch! What the . . . ." I can't finish my sentence. Pain shoots through my body when I put weight on my left foot.

The SUV's back door flies open. I see his shoes and smell the powerful signature scent before I raise my eyes.

Marcus O'Brien in the flesh. The man I loved for five years. My baby daddy. And now my nemesis.

"Carmela, are you okay? What are you doing with that bicycle?"

I stand on one foot. Balancing like a heron. I try to place my left foot back down but pain shoots up my spine. Tears border my lower lashes.

Don't you dare cry in front of him.

"Riding it," I snap to mask my pain.

His driver gets out and lights a cigarette. "Need help, boss?" Dark eyes flicker over me. Deciding I'm not important, he shifts his attention to the sky. "Rain is coming."

Where the hell does Marcus get these goons? He sure isn't from here.

A fat drop of water lands on my nose.

Really?

"Get in the car. These tropical storms are no joke," Marcus says commandingly as if I didn't survive a full force hurricane in the elements.

"Tell me about it," I grunt. I'd love to get to shelter. But I'm not taking a step in case I collapse in pain.

Where's Trixie when I need her? My trusty donkey would have trotted me home safely. Rain or no rain.

Marcus takes charge, picking up my bike with one hand and helping me hobble into the SUV with his other.

Raindrops the size of small stones pelt down on our heads.

The driver grabs my bike from Marcus and slides it into the cavernous trunk. Another man in the front seat asks if Marcus needs help.

At least that's what I think he asked. It was all guttural and deep and a tad bit scary.

The four of us sit in the SUV silently as the storm rages outside. It's no use driving in the sudden downpour. Even with the windshield wipers galloping a mile a minute, we can't see a thing outside.

Mist has descended shrouding the world in a white

cloud. Trees wave their branches wildly as if summoning help.

"I feel you," I whisper sympathetically to my beloved palms.

"We should take you to the hospital," Marcus says. "In case you sprained your ankle."

"And tell them you hit me with your fancy car."

Why am I being so bitchy? The man is offering to help.

Oh yeah, because he fired my fiancé. And canceled Christmas for the children. I shouldn't even be sitting in here.

I glance out the front window. The rain slaps the windshield like it's knocking some sense into the car.

A few more minutes of sheltering in a climate-controlled vehicle can't make a difference. It doesn't mean I'm caving.

"Carmela?"

With my arms folded, I mentally zip my lips, feeling childish but I don't care.

"Look, nothing I'm doing on St. Nicholas is meant to hurt you. I love you."

My eyes fly wide open. "What?"

"I . . . love . . . you." He stresses each word as if I'm four and not forty.

I so want to slap him and yell, "*snap out of it,*" like Cher did to Nicholas Cage in *Moonstruck*.

Even more reason to hug my arms to my body. In case one of them wants to try imitating art.

When I don't say anything, he continues talking about how he should have asked me to marry him on my birthday.

Thank God that you didn't. I wouldn't have found Keston.

"I made a mistake, Carmela."

Your first mistake is calling me Carmela.

He's never called me CJ, no matter how many times I've asked.

"We could be together. We could have a family with Lucy."

Is he delusional?

Through the mist, I see rain gushing down the hillsides creating new waterfalls and flooding the paths with muddy water.

Kind of what Marcus is doing to me. With his declarations of love and promises of a future. I'd have grabbed this offer nine months ago. His brown handsome face doesn't show a bit of regret.

I take him in from head to foot. Clean cut, hunter green polo showing off his gym-toned arms, long legs encased in premium linen that despite its hefty cost and air of elegance doesn't come close to the quality of Kelley's homespun hemp pants.

Part of me wants to ask him, "Why now?"

The other part wants to hurry up and get the hell out of this billionaire mobile before any of my new friends and soon to be family sees me fraternizing with the enemy.

"No thanks, Marcus. I'm all good."

Chapter Forty-Five

Except I'm not good!

The rain stops as abruptly as it started. The sun peeps out like a thespian at curtain call.

Then, as if seeing the coast is clear, the sun pushes the

clouds aside and beams down on us. "I'm here, sorry I had to take a break from all this shining and sparkling."

"About time," I grouch at the cheerful sunshine.

I ease out of the vehicle, hoping I'll be strong enough to pedal home.

Pain floors me as soon as I put my foot down. My dignity takes a nosedive as I cling to the car door weeping in pain.

Marcus rushes to my side. "Sweetheart let's go to the hospital. We need to get your foot x-rayed."

I nod. I'm in too much pain to argue. Or to point out that there's no "we." It's I who need my foot attended to.

He lifts me back inside the wide back seat and settles me down. I whimper at his touch. Not the good kind of whimper.

At the hospital, Marcus acts as if *he's* my fiancé. He explains that I twisted my ankle on the cobblestones. He leaves out the part about his driver hitting me with a SUV.

He tells the nurse I need premium care at whatever the cost and hovers nearby waiting for news.

"Your fiancé is so adorable," a male nurse says, patting my arm. "I wish I had a man like that."

"You can have him," I whisper under my breath.

It turns out my foot is worse than I thought. The doctor says it's a bad sprain. He gives me strong pain killers and wraps up my ankle to within an inch of my blood circulation.

I hear the doctor telling Marcus I need to rest. Marcus says to put me in the best room they have.

As if this is a hotel.

The doctor frowns at him. "All our rooms are suitable."

Marcus tilts his head. "We'll see."

Marcus better watch out. He can't *buy* the hospital.

Can he?

Ten minutes later, I'm wheeled into a private sunny room.

The male nurse hands me a bag of my personal effects. I grab my phone and call Keston.

"Baby, are you okay?" His deep voice overflows with emotions. "I was so worried. No one has seen you since you entered the library. I was beginning to think Mrs. Harris kidnapped you."

"She would, too. I have a lot to tell you. But first you should know I'm at the St. Nicholas Hospital."

"What!" His screech probably scared poor Trixie.

I explain the whole thing to him. How Marcus's SUV ran into my bike. How I fell and sprained my ankle. How the rainstorm appeared, and I had to seek shelter in his car. And how he brought me to the hospital.

Kes is silent on the other end.

"Are you there?" I turn the phone to see if I'm connected.

Keston's voice sounds far away. As if he's fading. Or maybe it's I who am fading away from the meds.

"How do you feel now?" I hear him say faintly.

"The room is nice," I slur. "It's not the Plaza."

"The what?" I can almost see his brow furrowing. "Never mind," he says. "I'm on my way."

"Okay." My eyes flicker shut. "See you soon."

I must have fallen asleep. When I open my eyes, it's to a loud ruckus in the hallway outside my room.

I hear shouts and whistles blowing and the sound of running feet. My heart beats wildly. What's going on?

My New York self trembles with fear. I struggle to sit up and swing my legs over the side of the bed.

Then I lean against the wall and half drag myself to the door to peep out.

What I see is unbelievable. I must be dreaming.

Except I doubt I'd ever dream that Keston Kips throws a right hook straight at Marcus O'Brien's face.

A full-blown fight is taking place in the hospital's hallway.

Marcus ducks but Kes's fist connects with Marcus's shoulder.

Bone on bone crackles and pops.

Ouch!

Marcus recovers and slams a fist into Keston's mid-section.

Keston grabs Marcus in a chokehold. Spins him around a few times like they're dancing, then tackles him to the floor.

"Cuff him, Loverboy," a familiar voice shouts.

"Smash him," another one says.

I peek around the doorway. Starr and Beast are holding back Marcus's driver and bodyguard.

As large and as highly trained as Marcus's men are, they're not as fearsome as St. Nicholas's fishermen who seem to be having a good time.

Getting physical is their everyday job. They fight waves, reel in large fish on lines, and pull nets every day. A fist fight must be nothing to them.

"Stop!" I shout. Except no one hears me over the grunting and yelling. Doctors and nurses stand back as the two men duke it out.

Don't they have hospital security here? Probably not. Why would they need any?

I look down at the hospital gown gaping open around my legs. If I could walk, I'd run over and break up the fight like Bridget Jones did when Mark Darcy and Daniel Cleaver were fighting over her on a London street corner.

At least Keston and Marcus aren't throwing each other through windows as they did in the movie.

Not yet. I glance around the hallway for any windows.

Keston and Marcus are about the same size. Marcus may be a wealthy man, but he grew up in the Bronx. He's not a stranger to fighting.

Keston looks mad as hell. He and Marcus fall apart. Keston scrambles to his feet and body slams Marcus to the shiny tiled floor.

Marcus's bodyguard struggles against Beast's vise grip. He isn't going anywhere.

This is horrible. Violence is not the answer.

My head is too fuzzy to think how to stop them. I hold on to the wall for dear life and pray for an intervention.

Chapter Forty-Six

"Did anyone call for help?" I try to raise my voice over the fracas. No one seems to hear.

Marcus gets up and crouches in the classic fight stance. "Is that all you got, island man?" He spits out.

Keston rolls his eyes. "I got everything. Stop hating."

Marcus lunges at Keston.

I scream.

Keston glances over at me, his eyes lighting up. Marcus punches twice, connecting first with Kes's jaw. Then with his eye. Blood spurts everywhere.

I scream louder.

Kes growls. "Get off my island," right before he dives on top of Marcus.

Both men go down like a ton of bricks.

I cover my eyes. "Please stop fighting."

At that moment, a voice shouts, "Enough!"

I open my eyes. It's Kelley. He strides down the hallway right into the melee and pulls the men apart single handedly.

He stretches both arms out, holding off the men, his face serene. "No more."

Marcus and Keston eye each other like two panthers in a forest.

"He hit CJ with his car," Keston snarls.

"Not on purpose, you idiot."

Kes makes to swing at Marcus again. Kelley grips his shirt. "No, brother."

"Yeah, listen to this guy." Marcus spits out blood.

A siren blares close by. Oh, Great.

Three officers enter walking fast toward the scene.

"What's up?" Kes nods at them.

"Is this the guy?" the one in charge asks Keston.

Keston nods again. "Yup. He's the one who hit CJ with his fancy car. Killed Christmas for all the kids and took over the Cocoa Reef Resort."

The head officer takes Marcus's arm. "You're under arrest."

"What for?" Marcus and his goons screech in unison.

Another of the officers gives a sardonic smile. "We don't let a Christmas Scrooge ruin our lives down here. No matter how much money they have."

Beast and Starr let go of the men in their grips.

"Don't forget these two," Beast says. "He punched me hard." Beast points to the bodyguard then at his chin. "It hurts." He rubs at it.

"You'll live Carlton," says the head officer.

I almost want to giggle at the look on Beast's face.

Tabitha runs down the hallway. I'm not sure where she's coming from. Her eyes are wild as she checks Kelley, then Keston before turning to Marcus.

"You're a monster. You used me. Then you come down here and fight my friends?"

He raises an eyebrow. "You got paid."

She slaps his face hard. It echoes down the hallway.

He looks up at the officer holding his arm. "You going to let her do that?"

The officer shrugs. "You finish hitting him, Miss Tabitha?"

Beast and Starr snicker like kids.

She nods.

Marcus looks at all of us. One by one. "You'll are crazy here. And you know what? I'm going to buy this whole damn island. Every square inch. Then I'll find that famous Kipson treasure and be even richer. None of you will have a home here any . . . ."

He doesn't get to finish.

Kelley Kips, the pacificist, the believer in non-violence, and unity, yanks Marcus away from the officer.

"No, you won't. Say you're sorry."

Marcus sneers. "Are you the dumb one?"

"No, I am," Keston says, reaching across Kelley to strike Marcus with the loudest punch.

Marcus crumples into a heap. His goons run to his side.

"Take him away," the lead officer says. "We don't want him here."

I watch all of this unfold, clinging to the doorknob. I'm shocked and unable to move.

I never realized that when they say the St. Nicholas islanders share everything, it means they share pain, too. How incredibly loyal.

No one, not the police officers, the hospital personnel, the fishermen, or the Department of Property (Tabitha) let Marcus or his men divide them.

Which makes me feel more blessed than ever because they accept me. I'm one of them.

Tabitha whisks past me. "This is all *your* fault," she snaps.

"Okay, well not *everyone* accepts me."

"She's just mad," Keston says, coming over, dried blood smeared across his cheek. One of his eyes is swelling shut.

"Who started the fight?" I ask, holding him off.

"He did, of course." Kes says, mildly. "When he came to St. Nicholas and tried to take my fiancée away."

"You can't fight everyone who shows an interest in me," I argue.

"Watch me," he growls.

I roll my eyes. "Promise me you won't."

"Okay, I promise."

"Well, that was quick."

He grins. "I'll get Beast to do it next time. He doesn't bruise."

I smack his arm. "Next time I'll beat you up myself."

"I didn't get beat up. It was a tie."

"Thank goodness for Kelley showing up."

Speaking of Kelley, I scan the hallways for my future brother-in-law. I want to make sure he's okay after Marcus called him dumb.

"Where's Kelley?" I ask.

Keston shrugs. "Probably making his cape."

"What?"

"You heard what Marcus said. He already bought the Cocoa Reef Resort. Now, he's threatened to buy everything on St. Nicholas. Kelley would fight to the death to save his home. And *our* home."

I shudder. "Let's hope no one has to fight anyone."

"Yes, let's. But we should have a Plan B."

I groan as Keston picks me up in his arms and walks me to the bed. He places me gently onto the cool sheets.

Without saying a word, he kicks off his shoes and climbs in next to me.

"What are you doing?"

"Staying with you, of course. The doctors said you can go home tomorrow." He wraps a warm, protective arm around my shoulders and pulls me close. "I'm not leaving you alone here with that lunatic running loose."

"What about Trixie?"

"She's fine. Kelley is taking her to his home."

"I've never been to Kelley's home and Trixie gets to go?"

"If you're a good girl, I'll take you one day."

I snuggle into his chest. "I'm always a good girl. It's you who's turned into a bad boy."

He presses his lips to my forehead.

"Do you think we can sneak in a quickie under the sheets?

"No!" I shiver as he slides a warm hand down my body.

"Okay, boss. Maybe tomorrow before we check you out."

"Maybe," I mumble as I fall into a deep sleep.

Chapter Forty-Seven

And just like that, it's the day before Christmas Eve. The day Mikah arrives. The day we're finalizing details on the Christmas huts.

Whenever I look out the cottage windows, I smile happily at the seven Christmas huts lined up on the beach.

Like the seven dwarves.

Each one is painted a different color and has its own personality: sky blue, pineapple yellow, lavender, sea green, sunset orange, mango red, and petal pink.

At the farthest end is the eighth and largest structure.

Lucy's, our brand-new beach bar, is finished.

Kelley painted *Lucy's* in a sparkling champagne color to meld with the sand and rocks. He carved the bar area from a huge piece of driftwood. He made bar stools out of trees that had fallen during the last hurricane.

Dex painted the stools in a rainbow of colors, and Kelley etched stars on them in honor of the celestial theme.

Each hut is covered with a thatched roof of palm leaves woven together tightly and tied down securely.

For the bar, Kelley has set up a sink and tank of fresh water and dug a pit to collect any runoff. He's given us an ecologically safe dish soap that does not pollute the water.

"Kelley," I told him when I tried it. "You can make a fortune with this soap."

He gave a rare smile. "I know."

"Well, why don't you?"

"I don't need a fortune," he said. And that was that.

I asked Keston one night, "Do you think Kelley might be another Einstein?"

He shrugged. "Could be."

When Kelley discovered we didn't have money to buy any alcohol to stock the bar, he showed up with bottles of dandelion wine and moonshine rum.

Keston had already bottled fruit juices and fresh spring

water and gathered every herb and condiment he needed for cocktails.

Captain Shaq donated a giant fish cooler that we've scrubbed and scrubbed until it is sparkling clean and free of any fishy smell.

As for stemware, *Lucy's* flyers say, "Bring a glass, leave a glass."

Kelley and Keston have also sanded and varnished a bunch of half-coconut shells to serve cocktails in. Our seaside *Lucy's* is as all-natural as you can get without being stranded on an island.

"Thanks, bro," Keston smacks Kelley on his shoulder, as they line the alcohol bottles side by side on the bar counter.

From my perch on Trixie's back, I admire how pretty the wines and rum look in their recycled bottles of many colors. I wouldn't be surprised if Kelley made the bottles too. I'm going to take a page from everyone's book and just assume he did and shrug it off.

"What's left to do?" Dex asks, sitting on one of the newly painted but dried stools.

Chapter Forty-Eight

I pull out my clipboard and rifle through the notebook pages.

Since Kelley hardly ever answers his phone except to take Mikah's calls, we have resorted to sharing notes the old-school way—by writing them down.

I sit on top of Trixie and ramble around the huts. My ankle hurts too much to walk, and Trixie has been happy to oblige and be my legs. Each morning, she waits patiently for me to climb up with Keston's help and she walks slowly so she doesn't jostle me.

I'm getting quite used to her sway-back stroll. I may never walk on my own legs again.

"Let me see," I say running my finger down the list.

I gently tap Trixie on her right side. "Let's go, boo."

She ambles along. I peek into each hut. The *Story Time* hut is decorated with pirate drawings I found in the chests that Keston grandmother, Viola Kips, left him. The same chests Mrs. Harris is dying to get her hands on.

The *Craft Hut* has bins of pretty shells and yarn, glue and glitter Tabitha collected from the sewing club.

The *Farm Hut* has pens for Kelley's goats and agoutis that he's bringing tomorrow. He's going to teach the kids how to take care of animals.

The *Game Hut* has puzzles, board games, soccer balls and badminton sets. Keston will set up the games on the beach and be the coach, referee and team leaders.

The *Fashion Hut* is stunning. It's Tabitha's masterpiece. She's brought trunks of clothing and accessories for anyone to play dress up and take selfies with the instant Polaroid camera donated by the Photo shop in town.

The *Food & Drinks Hut* is where all the children will be given their hotdogs and sandwiches, cupcakes and candy.

The men have strung solar lights around the tree trunks and the roofs of the huts.

"Everything is a go," I shout. "You guys should applaud yourselves. It's a miracle pulling it all off so fast."

Kes, Kelley, Dex and the fishermen beam up at me. They're passing around rum, drinking cold beers, or in Kelley's case, sipping mocktails and winding down for the day.

"The *Santa Hut* is the only problem. We still don't have a Santa."

Beast turns me down, as do Starr, Captain Shaq, and Redfish. They want to enter the boat races or give the kids boat rides.

No one wants to wear a heavy red suit, scratchy white beard, and a pom pom hat. Or walk around saying, *"Ho Ho Ho"* for hours. Even the promise of free drinks doesn't sway any of them.

"What are we going to do?" I wail. "Santa is *the* most important person at the Christmas party. The kids expect to see a Santa."

Keston, Dex, and Kelley will have their hands full coordinating the activities, the races, and all the food and drinks. They can't be Santa.

Trixie must hear the distress in my voice. She nuzzles my leg with her nose. "You can't be Santa, either sweetheart." I pat her soft ears.

"*Hee haw,*" she brays in agreement.

"*And* we don't have a Santa suit." I rub my chin.

"I can make one," Kelley offers.

"You're doing a lot. That's okay I'll figure it out."

I let Trixie take me to the porch, and I limp inside. I lay

on the bed and turn on the a/c. There's only one thing I can think of. I hope it's not too late.

Chapter Forty-Nine

"Mikah, it's me, CJ." I fix my hair on my phone screen.

Mikah is pink-cheeked and wearing a large poncho that would look terrible on anyone but her.

"You like it? It's a new designer. I want to show him some of Kelley's stuff."

"Good luck with that. Kelley doesn't sell anything."

"Right. I keep forgetting. I'll have to think of a way to barter it out of him."

I give a short laugh. "I'm excited to see you tomorrow, girl. But I have a favor to ask."

"More espresso capsules? I got you covered. Already packed."

"Thank you." I lean back on the pillows and look out the window. I can see the line of merry huts decorating our shoreline. When the sun goes down, twinkly solar lights will come on giving the entire scene a Christmas glow.

"I need a Santa suit."

"Pardon me."

"We have everything ready in time for the Christmas party. But no Santa. Or Santa suit."

Mikah eyes the suitcase opened on her bed. "You want me to stuff a Santa suit in there. No way it'll fit. And where would I get one?"

I slump. "That's the problem. Don't worry about it. I just wanted to cover all my bases."

"But what will you do?"

I scratch my arm where a mosquito tried to nibble some blood earlier. "I'll figure it out. You get here safely. See you tomorrow."

I can't wait to share the whole ordeal about Marcus and Keston and the big hospital fight. It was like a telenovela. Not the kind of thing you want to share over the phone.

After I hang up with Mikah, I check the time on my

phone. I want to call Lucy. We've been staying in touch regularly, chatting about school, her major, dating, roommates, and besties. Today, she's finishing her exams and flying home to Virginia. I want to wish her a safe trip home.

She answers my call in a cab on her way to the airport.

"Hi sweetie," I say.

"CJ, how are you? Marcus just told me he accidentally hit you with his car. He took you to the hospital. But that you're fine. It was a sprained ankle. Isn't it strange? My birth parents on the same tiny island and he hits her with a car?"

"Super strange. Like a movie."

"I'd say. A romcom? A thriller? What kind?"

More like a . . . ."

I can't imagine what kind of movie this life of mine would be.

"It's a mystery," I say truthfully.

We share a chuckle.

"How's the Christmas party plans?" she asks.

"Oh, pretty good. We're all set. Except for a Santa."

"What's wrong with the Santa?"

"We don't have one. Or a Santa suit."

The more I say it the more ridiculous it sounds to my ears.

"But the children will expect a Santa," she says.

"I agree. But what can I do?"

Before she can answer that, I say quickly. "Please don't worry about it."

"Too late. Have you asked all those cute fishermen you talk about?"

"They declined ever so politely."

Lucy grins. "What about a Mrs. Claus?"

Hmmm. "Maybe."

"I want to see lots of photos," she says. "Please."

"Maybe next year we could spend part of your Christmas vacation together," I suggest then hold my breath. Am I being too pushy?

"Absolutely," she says. "I'd love to. Plus, I must see *Lucy's*."

I laugh, forgetting my worries about a Santa. Lucy and I chitchat the rest of her way to the airport.

I hang up feeling my spirit renewed.

This is what it's like having a daughter. She can change your entire outlook.

My phone rings again. "Hi, did you forget to tell me something?" I ask cheerfully.

The person on the other end does not answer.

"Hello? Lucy? Is that you?"

"It's not Lucy," says a voice I don't recognize.

"Who is this?" I sit up. The hairs on the back of my neck raise.

"You will be sorry," says the voice. "You will be very sorry."

"Is this a joke? Who's going to be sorry?"

"Leave the island. And don't come back."

"For real. You have to do better than that, Giselle." I'm so sure it's my best friend pranking me, I hang up and call her right back. Aren't we too old for this?

"Hey CJ, what's up?" Giselle answers on the first ring confirming it was her.

"You tell me. Why'd you call me with that cheesy voice saying I'd better leave St. Nicholas?"

Giselle's face on the Facetime call is puzzled. "What are you talking about?"

"You called me," I insist. "A few seconds ago."

"No, I didn't. I was on the phone trying to order food when *you* called *me*."

"Oh." My hands tremble holding the phone. I tell Giselle what the caller said.

"Was it male or female?"

"I couldn't tell for sure."

We stare at each other. "I have a bad feeling," I say.

"Tell Keston right now. As a school principal, I urge you to take nothing for granted."

"Okay," I whisper. "I'll tell him."

But when I hobble out the bedroom, across the living room, and down the front steps in search of the crew, I find no one.

No Keston or his motorbike. No Kelley or his old/new truck. No fishermen or their boats. And no Dex managing the project.

Trixie trots over and scoots down so I can climb up. She is the smartest donkey in the world.

"Where is everyone?" I ask nervously.

"*Hee haw*," she brays loudly, trying to comfort me.

I usually feel a sense of peace and happiness here. Right now, my nerves are on edge.

"I'm not leaving the island, Trix. No one can make me." I look over my shoulder at the empty beach. Our boat bobs in the water next to the dock. The huts are lit up with the twinkly solar lights.

The sun sets fast into the sea. And the sky is ablaze with fiery colors.

Nope. I'm not going anywhere. I will, however, scold those men when they return.

"*Hee haw!*" she brays, louder this time. Like she plans to join me in doing so.

"Are you guys out of your minds?" I can't help getting a little shouty.

It's my nerves. I've been waiting to hear from them. Kes didn't answer his phone and Dex's phone went straight to voice mail.

Trixie and I have been star gazing to soothe our nerves. As fun as searching for constellations is in a night sky blanketed with stars, I'm worried sick about the guys.

And concerned for myself and Trixie!

With an ominous caller threatening God's knows what, and Marcus and his goons loose on St. Nicholas, I would like to know where my people are, thank you very much.

I pat Trixie pointy ears. "Not that you aren't great company."

She bares her teeth in a smile. Which makes me smile. Until she lets rip with a loud Trixie fart.

"It's a good thing I love you. Flaws and all."

She *hee haws* and settles next to me on the porch. I wonder if she knows she's not a dog.

I watch as the moon rises across the brightly lit sky. It shines a path of light on the sea. The palm trees sway, casting long leafy shadows on the shore. I can imagine what it must have been like hundreds of years ago when pirate ships sailed past here.

Or docked here more likely. Keston Kips's ancestor from the 1800s was a Pirate King and his son, whose mother was a Scottish noble woman married to the Governor, helped him buy all this land for as far as I can see. Helped in the sense she was able to get him deeds to the land.

This land was paid for with blood, sweat and a lot of pirate booty.

Now billionaire Marcus O'Brien, with no ties to St. Nicholas, wants it all.

He can't have it. I vowed to Keston we would never sell his land.

I doze off on the porch, stroking Trixie's ears and dreaming of the pirates and the treasures they stole. Treasures that were stolen in the first place by conquistadores from the Incas in Peru.

I awake when I hear the roar of Keston's motorbike and the purr of Kelley's truck.

I jump off the porch swing and greet them, hands on hips, foot tapping, mouth pursed.

Kes gets off clutching a bouquet of wildflowers wrapped in one of his bandanas. Like that's going to make things better. Ha!

I scowl harder. "They look familiar. Did you steal them from the Cocoa Reef Resort?"

He doesn't need to answer. I recognize the beautifully planted flowers that decorated the walkways of the resort.

"For you, baby.

"Are you crazy? You went to the resort?

"We had to baby. We have a surprise?"

"I'm mad."

"At me?" He grins.

"God, yes, can't you at least look upset that I'm mad?"

Kelley follows Kes with Dex in tow. They're carrying something that's a very bright red color.

I stare in disbelief at what they're holding. "What did you guys do?" I demand.

"We got you what you needed," Keston says.

He proudly takes the bright red Santa suit, trimmed with white fur and belted with a wide black belt, from Kelley and holds it up proudly.

Dex clutches a pair of shiny black boots fit for a giant.

Kelley spins a red fur Santa hat with white trim and a black pompom around and around on his fingers.

My eyes widen. "Are you kidding me? Where did you get this?"

The men exchange looks.

"We stole it," Dex admits.

"Borrowed," Kelley corrects.

"From the Cocoa Reef Resort," Keston explains. "I knew where the Food Manager kept it. It was easy to sneak in and grab it. No one will notice it's missing. We only need it for two days."

Kelley nods. "We *will* put it back."

"But now you have everything," Dex says. "You can check it off your list."

I try to hide my shock at their foolishness.

I can't. "Suppose Marcus saw you," I shout at Keston. "It would have been another fight. And this time you'd be on his private property."

Keston and Dex snort at the same time.

I want to remind them that Marcus *bought* it. And that this isn't one of those 'share everything' scenarios. But I can't throw that in their faces. They lost their jobs there.

"Thank you," I say grudgingly. "The suit is perfect. If we don't get

arrested for 'borrowing' it.

Keston scoffs "Who's going to do that?"

He has a point. The St. Nicholas Islanders police officers went to school with Keston. Their loyalty is golden.

"We still don't have a Santa." I eyeball the Santa suit for size.

"We're working on that," says Dex.

"For now," Kes adds, "everything is taken care of. You can relax. We will pick up Mikah tomorrow and then put the last-minute touches on everything. I promise you; we'll find someone to go *Ho Ho Ho*!"

I sigh. "That's a relief. But we have another problem."

Three sets of eyebrows fly up. "What is it?" Kelley asks.

I wring my hands as I tell them about the caller and the threats. "He or she told me to leave the island and don't come back."

"That's bullshit," Keston says forcefully.

"Sounds like a desperate person," Kelley says. "Why would anyone be desperate for you to leave?"

"I don't know."

But then Mrs. Harris's suspicious eyes flash across my mind. Her determination to find the pirate treasure could make her want to threaten me. Since she believes I have something of value from Viola Kips, Keston's grandmother.

Which I do have. In the form of an ancient diary.

But Kelley has another diary. Which no one knows about. Not even his estranged mother.

"Do you have any idea *who* it could be?" Keston asks gently.

I give a tiny shake of my head. The truth is, I can't believe how *many* it could be.

I have a growing list of people who don't want me on St. Nicholas. Tabita St. Clair. Marcus O'Brien. And now Mrs. Harris.

Chapter Fifty-One

We end the night on a solemn note. Each of us wrapped up in our own thoughts.

Dex is focusing on finding a Santa. Kes and I discuss the identity of the mysterious caller. And Kelley stares out to sea, probably inventing some new form of energy from the rolling waves.

After eating a simple meal of fried fish and seaweed salad, Kelley drops Dex home and comes back to our house to spend the night.

I put a pillow and blanket in the porch hammock for him. Kes and Kelley smile at my plumping up Kelley's pillow.

"What?" I ask. "We don't have to be animals, do we?"

Trixie snorts loudly as if saying, "Why not?'

We have a laugh breaking the tension for the moment.

"Let's get some sleep. Tomorrow will be amazing." Kes nods at his brother and leads me away.

But I can't sleep.

Keston and I make love quietly. Our bodies know each other's so well.

We slide together in a perfect dance, his legs intertwining with mine, his hips pressing against mine and finally his sweet cock sliding into my wet and waiting pussy.

We move as one -- slowly, leisurely -- until I feel a familiar wave of desire hit my stomach. It expands outwards like the sun's rays lighting me up.

I grip his shoulders, wrap my legs around his waist and grind my hips against his, pulling him deep inside. We rock back and forth as one.

"I love you, woman," he whispers.

"You love *it*."

"I do."

We giggle, panting and bucking our hips perfectly in time with each other.

I gasp at the moment of our sweet release.

Afterwards, as we lay wrapped up together, I whisper, "You're the last man I'll ever sleep with." It's my promise of utmost fidelity for him and myself.

His arm around my shoulders loosens. "What about women?"

"The last man *or woman*, sheesh."

"Thank you, much better."

"What about you?" I ask, poking his muscled arm. "Aren't you going to say it?"

"I'm already doing it."

"Cool." I kiss his chest.

I throw a leg over his and snuggle closer. I stare at the moon outside the bedroom window. It seems to wink at me off and on as my eyelids slide down into a dreamless sleep.

"CJ!"

It's my mother's voice. "Wake up!"

What is my mother doing here?

Why is she shaking me?

"Now!" My mother says. "Wake up!"

It's strange how mothers can be everywhere with you even when you can't see them. It's like what Kelley said. Certain people are part of your soul. You don't have to miss them. They are always with you. Which is why I'm hearing my mother's voice full of warning ringing in my ears.

"CJ!"

I snap open my eyes.

"What?"

The smell of kerosene fills my nostrils. Strange orange light flickers outside the window.

Keston is not in the bed.

I jump up confused. Why is it so bright outside?

I'm trying to make sense of what I'm seeing, thinking it's a dream, when Keston rushes back in.

I pinch him.

'Ouch, get dressed."

I scramble up. "What's going on?"

Keston's face is grim.

I stare blankly at him. My brain is trying to block out what my senses know.

Our world outside is on fire. I can see the flames from here. I can smell the burning. My heart is gripped with a fear so immense I can't move.

"Where's Kelley?" I whisper.

Keston moves quickly, dropping one of his tee shirts over my head. It hangs to my knees. He's a tall man.

He gives me the briefest hug. "We have to go."

I nod and pull up a pair of shorts.

To Keston, I yell, "I'm coming."

He hesitates in the doorway.

"I'm fine," I assure him. "Check on Kelley. And Trixie."

One glance out the window says it all. Our Christmas huts are ablaze.

Kelley's hard work. Keston and Dex's labor. Our

Christmas market for the kids. All of it is burning up. My heart cracks wide open.

My mother's voice in my head shouts, "CJ, you have to move now!"

Her voice flips my *On* switch!

"Okay. Mom," I say in my head.

I race outside to see Trixie trotting away from the blaze. She's headed down the dirt road. Thank goodness.

She stops and turns around when she hears my footsteps. "Go girl," I shout and wave her on. "Go be safe."

The air on the front porch is smoky. But the breeze is blowing most of the smoke out to sea.

I run over to help Kelley and Keston haul buckets of water from our tanks. It's like pouring a cup of water on the Empire State Building. Our buckets aren't making a bit of difference.

The books and drawings burn, filling the air with ash. The games and toys burn, emitting a strong and acrid odor.

The fire eats at the wooden huts, one by one, in a dance of flames.

"No," I cry. "This can't be happening."

The fire is licking up one wooden structure after another in rapid succession. The wind is blowing the flames away from our home, but toward the beach bar.

"We have to stop it before it gets to the bar," Kelley shouts. "The alcohol will explode."

Oh my God. All that high-proof moonshine and wine. If it explodes, the fire will spread everywhere. The house, the trees, everything will burn.

I rush toward the gorgeous wooden bar as Keston and

Kelley try to push the entire tank of water toward the fire. It's impossible. The tank is too big. It's too heavy, filled to the brim with rainwater from the heavy rains we had recently.

I look around for something, anything that will stop the fire.

"CJ, get away from there," Keston shouts. His face and arms are streaked with soot. His voice is hoarse from the smoke.

Kelley jumps in his truck. He reverses and then heads straight for the tank.

"What is he doing?" I shout.

Keston and I watch as Kelley backs up again and repositions the truck.

"I think he's trying to tip over the tank by hitting it with his truck," Keston says. Kelley drives toward the tank at top speed from a different angle. He

hits the giant plastic tank with a loud bang.

"Oh my God, that must hurt. Make him stop," I yell.

But Kelley isn't listening to us.

He backs up his truck again.

I run to the beach bar and scoop up sea water with a bucket. If I wet the area around the bar maybe the fire won't spread.

Another loud bang tells me Kelley has rammed the tank again.

At that moment I hear Trixie's bell approaching. She's come back?

I look around wildly.

"Trixie?"

"*Hee haw*," she brays over and over. It sounds like she's crying.

Please don't tell me she's come back for me.

I'm still scooping up sea water and running with the bucket toward the beach bar. The intense heat from the encroaching flames burns my nostrils.

"CJ," Kes shouts. "Get away from there."

I turn to leave with my bucket just as I see Trixie sticking her nose into the last hut. The one next to the bar. She *is* looking for me.

"Trixie, come here," I cry. "Now!"

She turns her head left and right, looking confused. Smoke shifts and covers her grey body. I can't see her, but I hear the little bell tinkling.

And then she starts to cry even louder. I run toward her cry.

"Trixie," I cough as smoke hits my lungs.

"CJ, no," I hear Kes screaming my name.

But I'm not letting my donkey burn to death. It's only because she loves me that she came back for me.

I push aside the thatch roof leaves falling to the sand. It's the last hut before the bar. The sound of wood cracking and falling apart is deafening.

"Trixie," I cough. Smoke swirls around my head at the entrance of the burning hut.

A wall of fire appears. It's falling in slow motion. Tipping straight toward me. I scream. Trixie cries pitifully.

A strong hand yanks me backward and tosses me to the sand.

It's Keston.

He's hitting me, punching me, rolling me around on the sand.

"Dude," I try to shout. But no words come out. My mouth is full of smoke and sand.

What the hell is he doing?

Pain shoots through my arms as Keston smacks them over and over, probably getting me back for all the times I've smacked his arms.

It takes me a minute to realize I'm on fire. He picks me up and runs into the sea, dunking me under the water like I'm being baptized.

I come up sputtering in his arms.

At that moment, Trixie runs out of the hut and straight toward us. She splashes through the shallow water moaning.

"Fuck," Keston shouts.

I stare in horror as the fire beelines for the beach bar.

And there outlined in the smoky blaze is Kelley revving his truck straight for the bar. He's pulling a thick rope. It's tied around the tank.

Instead of trying to push it over, he's pulling it, dragging it slowly but surely toward the burning bar, his tires rolling over the firey wood.

"No!" I shout. "He's driving into the inferno."

Keston and I cling to each other in shock.

Chapter Fifty-Two

As a lawyer, I know the significance of using the right words to persuade a jury or a judge, a client or an opposing counsel.

But I've never thought much about using the right words with myself. I try to use positive words. I try to believe in myself. And I try my best at whatever I do.

But that's my problem. The word, "try."

It embraces the possibility of failing. Sure, anyone can fail at something, but when you say you're going to "try," you automatically give yourself a way out. You sugar coat your determination. You basically open the door to the expression heard so often, "*Well, I tried.*"

Those are my thoughts as I swim against the current toward our boat on the dock. To my utter surprise, Trixie swims next to me, keeping her head above water.

"You can swim? Who knew that?"

Trixie is first to the boat. I drag myself up on the dock after her, panting to catch my breath.

I don't have much time.

Right before Kelley's truck slammed into the beach bar, dragging the tank of water behind it, Keston took my shoulders and said, "CJ, you need to swim to the boat. Keys are under the driver's mat. Bring the boat here. Turn it around like you've seen me do and back in as close as possible to the shore. Watch the waves. Don't let them swamp you."

I stared at him as waves lapped around our shoulders. "I can't do that."

"You can do anything. I've witnessed it."

"But I can't turn your boat around and back it up."

Keston wasn't listening. He was jumping over the waves heading back to the beach. Back to our burning beach bar. Back to Kelley.

I whimpered.

"I'll try," I shouted at his retreating back.

"Babe, forget try. Do it."

I tie Trixie to a dock post with a piece of rope. "Stay here, you're safe."

She lays down, her eyes on me as I search for the boat key and stick it into the ignition.

She gives a little "hee haw," when the boat starts with a rumble.

I jump out and untie the ropes, then leap back in, just as I've seen Keston do.

"I'm doing this," I mutter to myself, guiding the boat away from the dock. It's not easy. I bump the dock a few times.

"I'm not trying. I'm *doing*," I repeat the mantra.

My brain may believe I lack boating skills, but I'm not listening to that organ. I'm listening to my heart.

My heart says, "You can do this."

My soul says, "You can do this."

I say, "You can do this!"

I take deep breaths and focus on the water; I watch the waves. I count the way they're rising and falling.

How often have I watched these waves from the front porch? They rise and fall in a pattern. Three waves then the sea flattens out for a minute before the waves start again.

That space when the water flattens out is my spot. That's when I'll turn the boat around and back into shore.

I motor parallel to the shore in water deeper than where the waves are breaking. So far, so good.

I can see the fire dying down on the beach. Kelley managed to drag the water tank to the beach hut and tip it over. But not before he drove into the fire and risked his life.

Wham! A big wave comes out of nowhere. The boat shuts off. I frantically turn the ignition. It's not re-starting.

Oh God. All my lofty thoughts about doing and not trying has got me stranded.

I wasn't watching the water. I know better. Never turn your back on the sea.

The boat drifts. I turn the key in the ignition. Nothing.

I must let it sit for a moment. But another wave is coming. It's heading straight toward me.

I wait and wait, my heart in my throat. I'm the only chance we have of getting Kelley to a hospital. His truck is destroyed. Keston cannot ride him on his motorbike. It's up to me.

I watch the wave getting closer. I watch it rise, watch it curve, the sheer size of it terrifies me.

I know what I must do.

I turn the key gently. Pray the engine kicks in. It does!

Then, I fly like the wind under the wave. Tunneling through the wall of water like I'm Kelly Slater on his surfboard.

I beat the wave. When I'm close to shore, I spin the boat around so I'm facing the oncoming wave.

It takes all my courage to keep the boat steady as the wave breaks across the bow. The water splashes into the boat, soaks me, and then drains away.

If I hadn't maneuvered the boat as I did, using pure instincts, me and the boat would have been eaten by that wave.

I hear a cheering from the beach. "Way to go, CJ. Now back it up."

I look over my shoulder and steer the boat toward the shore, keeping one eye on the water in front. It's the quiet time. We have one minute.

Keston wades toward the boat carrying Kelley in his arms. Kelley's head lolls to the side. His hair is covered with ash, his skin looks blackened. I reach over and help bring in the heavy limp body.

Kelley groans loudly. His face is distorted with pain.

My heart goes out to him. Nothing is more important right now than saving Kelley's life.

I close my eyes and start praying.

Keston hauls himself into the boat and grabs the steering wheel. He pushes the throttle all the way up and we blast off before another wave can douse us.

I sit on the long seat, holding Kelley's head on my lap.

"Where're we going?" I shout over the wind.

"Cocoa Reef Resort."

It's our closest neighbor. They have a medic on call. But more importantly, they have a helicopter.

Chapter Fifty-Three

Marcus may be a rich jerk, but he's no monster. He'd noticed the smoky sky and the flames over our land and had a boat and boat pilots on standby ready to investigate and help.

When we zoom up to the Cocoa Reef dock, Marcus's

men are waiting. They put Kelley in a golf cart. I climb up on the back seat.

Keston says he's going back to make sure the fire is out and wait for the fire department. He'll see us at the hospital.

"Don't forget Trixie is tied to the dock," I tell him.

He nods tersely. The strain of the evening is all over his face.

One of the resort's security guards, who is a St. Nicholas islander, jumps in the boat and says he'll help out Keston, for which I am grateful.

At the front of the resort, we transfer to Marcus's cavernous SUV.

I'm terrified at Kelley's utter silence. I'd rather he was groaning or something. I put my finger under his nose to make sure he's still breathing.

The rest of the night is a blur.

Once at the hospital, I call Dex and Tabitha.

Dex says he'll catch a ride to our home to see if Keston needs him.

"He needs you," I cry.

Tabitha rushes into the hospital waiting room crying, no make-up, clothes disheveled. We cling to each other as I sob out the story.

You know shit is bad when I'm crying on Tabitha's shoulder.

Now that I'm safe and the adrenaline has worn off, my entire body shakes like a leaf in a storm.

"You're wet," Tabitha points out.

She grabs a passing nurse and asks her to admit me. Next thing I know I'm in a hospital gown and hooked up to an IV.

I feel foolish being wheeled down the corridor for the second time in one week. I can only hope the hospital personnel don't recognize me as the woman who caused a fist fight in their hallways.

I'm wheeled into the same room. Put in the same bed. Apparently, I have minor burn marks on my arms and back. The nurse treats them, wraps them up and gives me some antibiotics.

My eyes are fighting to stay open. But I refuse to give in to sleep. Not until I hear how Kelley is doing.

"He's going to be okay, isn't he?" I cry deliriously to Tabitha.

We're holding hands. She nods vigorously. "Yes. He's Kelley Kips."

Then she tells me story after story of Kelley's amazing feats growing up. From building a slide from the top of his house all the way down the cliff to the sea, to starting a beehive and creating a special honey that can only be found on St. Nicholas.

"It has healing properties," she says.

"We need to get some," I murmur. "For his wounds."

"We will."

"Tabitha," I whisper. "Do you think Gang Gang Sarah did this?"

"What? Why?"

I tell her how I fell on her grave. "Keston told me she's a witch and can put a curse on us and we'd need an obeah man or woman to break it."

Tabitha purses her lips. "Gang Gang Sarah would not hurt Kelley Kips. Or Keston. You, however, maybe."

My brows draw in. "Really?"

She shakes her head. Smiles wickedly. "Nah. But it's nice for me to think so."

I roll my eyes. "You know I'm not going anywhere, right?"

She nods. "You're kind of growing on me."

I must have fallen asleep. Because when I open my eyes again, the sun is up, and streaming into the room like a reminder that a new day brings new life.

Chapter Fifty-Four

The first thing I do is pray. For all of us. But mostly for Kelley. I pray so hard my eyeballs hurt from squinching them together. My fingers hurt from clenching them.

"Can I join you?" It's a voice I hold dear.

"Mikah," I cry.

She rushes to my side.

"That guy Alex picked me up from the airport again."

"In his purple low rider?"

She nods. "He's a decent man. Why is he still single?

I shake my head. "I don't know. But I can find him a match and *True Love Trips* them one day."

We sit side by side on my bed. Mikah's face is teary. Her eyes blood shot. As if she's been crying for a while.

My heart races.

"Have you heard anything?"

"I can't . . . ."

"What?" My heart caves. "How is Kelley?"

She shakes her head. Wipes her nose with a tissue. "He's in ICU," she says somewhat calmly.

"Okay." I sigh.

Then her cool demeanor is gone.

She stands up. Paces back and forth, gesticulating with her hands. Raising her voice. "What was he thinking? How could he do something so dangerous? How could he risk his life? I hate him. I love him. I can't do this."

She collapses on the bed next to me. I rub her back. Even though my arms are killing me. "Shhh," I whisper. "We are going to do this together."

And that's what happens.

The entire St. Nicholas community rises and comes together. The hospital is flooded with visitors for Kelley Kips.

Word of Kelley's bravery flew like hummingbirds around the island. News about how he worked tirelessly to give the

St. Nicholas children a Christmas party. And how he saved our land. How he saved our lives.

Tabitha organizes the visitors into groups because they are too many at once. All the people who've shunned Kelley most of his life arrive with flowers, fruits, home remedies for burns. Special healing powders, drinks, potions and more.

Mrs. Harris comes, crying like a baby. The cool aloof woman breaks down in the waiting room so Tabitha brings her to my room.

"Carmela, how can I make this right?" she cries, tears seeping through her fingers as she covers her face with her hands.

"You're his mother," I say gently. "You just need to be there. The rest will come. Don't over think it. Don't be afraid."

She nods. I can't believe I'm giving advice about mothering.

But when Lucy calls to see if I am okay, because Marcus had called her, I cry too. "I'm okay, sweetie. I'm fine. How are you?"

She rattles off a list of things she's doing to get ready for Christmas. She ends with, "I'm so glad we found each other. I want you to know, you didn't need to be afraid twenty years ago. You are the strongest woman I know. I'm glad you are my birth mother."

We hang up and I bawl my eyes out.

Mrs. Harris looks worried. I wave my hand in the air like this is nothing.

"Go see Kelley," I urge. "You're allowed in the ICU. Family only. Keston has been up there since this morning."

She blanches. "Keston?"

"Yes, Keston. He's Kelley's brother. You're Kelley's mother. Now go."

Mrs. Harris gets up, squeezes my hand, and thanks me. "You're one in a million, Carmela Jones."

I smile weakly. "So, I've been told."

She squares her shoulders. "Do you think he'll forgive me?"

"They just want to know we love them. It's not hard."

"What about the mistakes I made?"

"It's never too late to step up and repair those." I smile thinking of Lucy's last words. I will live and die by them forever.

"Hopefully, not die," I whisper to Gang Gang Sarah. "I've got a lot more stuff to do here."

Chapter Fifty-Five

One week later, I'm sitting with my new family in Kelley's hospital room. There's Kelley and Mikah, Tabitha, Dex, Keston and me.

It's midnight and the old year is changing over to a new one.

We're *oohing* and *aahing* at the New Year's Eve fireworks lighting up the St. Nicholas Island sky. We blow our horns and throw our sparkly hats into the air.

It's all thanks to Marcus who imported a pyrotechnic team to delight his guests at the Cocoa Reef Resort.

I can't believe Marcus is still here. But it seems as if he's making the island his winter base. He says the islanders surprise him with their kindness. He feels at home.

Marcus grew up in foster care. He's not used to people having his back for no reason.

But the islanders have no interest in his wealth and no qualms about telling him the truth and hurting his feelings. Something he's not used to.

Which is what happened on December 23rd after the fire.

Everyone let Marcus know he had ruined their children's Christmas. And now that our plans had gone up in smoke – literally -- they told Marcus he had to host the party.

The way it had always been. At the Cocoa Reef Resort.

If Marcus was daunted that he had 24 hours to plan and execute a Christmas party, with toys and a Santa, he did not show it.

Instead, he hired Tabitha and Dex. Paid them a lot of money. Gave Tabitha a limitless credit card and use of his helicopter.

Tabitha says it was the most fun she's ever had in her life. I've seen the party photos. It was a rousing success.

Guess who was Santa?

Not the Food Manager as before. Tabitha insisted that the only way people would forgive Marcus for canceling the party and golf tournament was to wear the Santa suit and be the white-bearded old man the children loved.

And he did it.

This makes me wonder, is there more to Tabitha and Marcus's relationship? Because Marcus would not have dressed up as Santa for me! Or for anyone.

The thing with tragedies or natural disasters is that they bring people together. They tend to highlight the close connection we all share as humans.

We feel for another person's pain or loss. We lose and we gain. The circle of life.

As I sip my tiny glass of champagne and reminisce about the past year of life-changing events, I smile at each member of my new family.

Kelley is covered in bandages but recovering with the help of a team of burn specialists that Marcus flew down to reconstruct Kelley's beautiful body.

"You were way too handsome to begin with," I tease him. "Gotta bring your beauty down a notch."

His eyes shine at me. "I can always count on CJ for the truth."

"She's right," Mikah says, sitting on the edge of Kelley's bed. Their hands are intertwined. "I want to be the pretty one in this relationship."

Keston's arms are wrapped loosely around me, so he

doesn't hurt my shoulders that are still healing. "Bro," he says. "Don't listen to these ladies. We Kips men are the pretty ones."

Dex hoots a laugh. "I'd say. I've seen women go crazy for this one." He points a thumb at Keston.

"Shhh," Kes says. "That was the past."

I smack his arm. He's the only one who did not suffer any injuries. How in the world he dove into the fiery mess to save Kelley and did not get burned at all has me wondering.

Is he magical? Does he have special powers?

When I'd asked him that a few days ago, he'd demonstrated his "special powers" with his tongue.

"We're in the hospital!" I screeched as he parted my legs.

"And?"

"The nurse can walk in."

He winked. "I put a 'Do Not Disturb' sign on the door."

"Hospitals do not have 'Do Not Disturb' signs," I protested.

He smirked. "I made one. Trixie helped. She marked it with a moody hoof."

"You're incorrigible."

"And you're delicious."

He sucked my pussy like I was a juicy mango. My nipples hardened. My eyes closed and I shamelessly begged for more.

I plan on carrying his 'Do Not Disturb' sign wherever we travel.

For the entire week, none of us have spoken about the fire. It's as if we didn't want to jinx Kelley's recovery by mentioning the cause.

But now, with the fireworks creating magic in the sky, we delve into it.

Mostly because Keston received the fire inspector's preliminary report, and he wants to share it with us.

"It doesn't make sense," he growls. "The footsteps found at the scene are made by foreign boots. The kerosene bottles are labeled in Spanish. And someone dropped a pack of matches."

"From where?" Kelley asks.

Keston shakes his head. "From no place I've ever heard of."

Mikah asks to read the report. She looks at the photos intently. No one else knows she's been a spy for twenty years.

After Dex says his goodbyes to head back to his family, we huddle together.

"What are you not telling us, Mikah?" I ask.

She grips the photo of the matches. "I've seen these before. In real life."

"When?" I ask.

"How?" asks Kelley.

"Where did you see them?" Keston wants to know.

Mikah looks at each of us. As if preparing to drop a bomb.

My heart hopscotches across my chest.

"Tell us."

"Guys, these footprints, kerosene bottles, and especially these matches belong to a notorious group of pirate treasure hunters that hang out in the Eastern Nile region of Africa.

"Pirate treasure hunters?"

"Africa?"

"Speak plainly," Tabitha jumps in.

"This group of pirate treasure hunters is extremely dangerous. They travel the globe seeking lost pirate treasure. They're extremists. They claim to be restoring the riches to the rightful owners. And they destroy anyone or anything that gets in their way. Arson is their weapon of choice."

I suck in the air and choke. Kes pats my back gently. "Easy baby."

"You think these pirate hunters are here?" I ask terrified.

"It seems they have their eyes set on St. Nicholas."

"The scary phone call," I whisper. "The person had an accent."

Mikah nods. "I don't know much. Cause it's your secret. But you might want to safeguard any treasure you've found. Before the pirate hunters steal it away."

Kelley, Keston, Tabitha, and I exchange looks.

Just when I thought the coast was clear and I could live happily ever after on a beach with my man and a cute donkey.

Starting a new business. Rebuilding our beach bar. And most of all, planning a wedding of my dreams.

Wrong!

Now, we've got to find the lost Kipson treasure before some extremists do.

I look around at our little family. "Who's in?" I whisper.

Tabitha scoffs. "Do you even have to ask, CJ?"

"You know I'll go wherever you want me to, baby," Keston says, nuzzling my neck.

I bite my lip and look at Kelley. He's in a lot of pain. How can I ask him to risk his life again?

"I was born for this," he says evenly. "Finding the Kipson treasure was the *reason* my mother and our father had me." He nods at Keston.

"Can I help?" Mikah asks, jumping in. "If Kelley was born for this, I've *trained* for this. Literally."

"Hell yeah," I high-five my friend. "You're one of us now, aren't you?"

Mikah smiles shyly, brushing her long hair aside. "I don't know. It's up to him."

Kelley's eyelids flutter down. Despite his holding hands with Mikah, I still don't know how he feels about her. And apparently, neither does Mikah.

"We have time to figure it out," Keston says. For now, "Happy New Year! Here's to CJ becoming my bride."

I laugh and raise my tiny glass. "We're going to need a lot more bubbly for that to happen."

"Bubbly for the Bride," Keston says, kissing my nose. "I'm on it."

I mentally count my blessings for the new year, starting with the best of all: I've found my one true love. Now, all I have to do is marry him.

The End!

Book 4, *Bubbly for the Bride* will be next🤍

Lynn Joseph is from Trinidad & Tobago. When she's not writing her international romances, she can be found on a beach somewhere in the world. Or binge-watching *Hart of Dixie* and *The Vampire Diaries* over and over. Lynn lives in charming South Portland, Maine, and on the Caribbean Island of Tobago, where she's known as the Mermaid Queen. Join her on her journey of love, food, and romantic destinations (not necessarily in that order). www.lynnjoseph-books.com

Also by Lynn Joseph

The Walker Sisters Forever Series

(Sweet Romance)

Gelato Forever

Olives Forever

Sangria Forever

Paris Forever

Christmas Forever

Cocoa Reef Resort Series

(Steamy Romance)

Lime to My Coconut

Rum to the Reggae

Spice for My Santa

Princess Abroad

(Read for FREE! —> https://BookHip.com/NKSQGRS)